# Through the Lens of Us

Lena Snow

Published by Lena Snow, 2024.

THROUGH THE LENS OF US

**First edition. September 17, 2024.**

Copyright © 2024 Lena Snow.

ISBN: 979-8227963444

Written by Lena Snow.

# Chapter 1:

As I stepped into my room, the grandeur of the villa seemed to seep into every corner. The suite was bathed in soft sunlight filtering through billowy curtains, and I could hear the distant murmur of the ocean waves. The room had a private terrace overlooking the sprawling blue expanse, the kind of view that would make anyone's heart skip a beat. I let out a breath I didn't realize I was holding and took a moment to absorb the beauty around me. This was the calm before the storm, and I needed to be ready.

I unpacked quickly, my hands still slightly trembling, and made my way back downstairs to the courtyard. The crew was busy setting up equipment, their voices a blend of focused chatter and laughter. I watched them for a moment, trying to gauge the atmosphere, to understand how I would fit into this well-oiled machine.

Then, there was a commotion near the entrance, and I saw him for the first time. Liam Hudson. He walked in with an effortless grace, his presence commanding the attention of everyone in the room. He was even more striking in person—tall and impeccably groomed, with an aura that seemed to make the air around him crackle with energy. The moment he stepped into the courtyard, the conversation hushed, and all eyes were on him.

He glanced around, his gaze fleeting but sharp. I could feel the weight of his scrutiny even from a distance, and my heart raced. I tried to steady myself, reminding myself of the professionalism I had promised to uphold. This was my chance to prove myself, and I couldn't let my nerves get the best of me.

Liam's eyes finally landed on me. There was a moment of stillness where our gazes met, and in that instant, I felt a jolt of something—anticipation, perhaps, or the first hint of fear. His expression was unreadable, a mask of detached curiosity. I offered a

1

tentative smile, but he simply nodded and turned his attention back to the crew.

"Liam, this is Ava Green," Giuseppe said, his voice cutting through the tension. "She's our photographer for the month."

Liam's gaze shifted back to me, and he extended a hand with a practiced politeness that barely masked the indifference in his eyes. "Nice to meet you, Ava."

His handshake was firm but brief, and I had the distinct feeling that he was sizing me up. I managed to return his greeting with a smile that I hoped was confident. "Nice to meet you, Liam. I'm looking forward to working together."

He gave a curt nod and turned away, heading towards the area where the first set of shots would be taken. I watched him walk away, a strange mix of awe and anxiety swirling inside me. This was not going to be easy, but I was here to do a job, and I intended to do it well.

The first day of the shoot passed in a whirlwind of activity. Liam posed with an air of practiced ease, but there was an underlying tension in his movements, a constant reminder that he was a man accustomed to control. I tried my best to capture the essence of his charisma without letting his demanding nature overshadow my work. Each click of the camera felt like a small victory, a step towards proving myself in this high-stakes environment.

As the day wound down, I retreated to the quiet of my room, my mind racing. The villa was serene in the evening light, the sound of the waves a soothing backdrop to my thoughts. I reviewed the shots from the day, searching for any signs of the elusive connection I hoped to capture. It was clear that Liam was a master of his craft, but the challenge was getting past his veneer of professionalism to reveal something more authentic.

My phone buzzed with a message from a friend, a comforting distraction from the day's stresses. We exchanged a few lighthearted texts, and I found solace in the normalcy of our conversation. It was a reminder that despite the glamour and pressure of this shoot, I was still just Ava Green, a photographer with a dream.

I went to bed that night with a mix of exhaustion and excitement. Tomorrow would bring new challenges, new opportunities to connect with Liam Hudson and to show him—and myself—what I was capable of. As I drifted off to sleep, I clung to the hope that this experience would be more than just a professional milestone. It was my chance to step into a world I had only ever dreamed of, and no matter how daunting the path, I was ready to take it.

His hand was warm and firm as it wrapped around mine, and for a brief second, I felt the faintest spark of connection—a tiny, unexpected crack in his carefully crafted facade. I tried not to dwell on the fleeting moment, focusing instead on maintaining my composure.

"Nice to meet you, Liam," I managed, hoping my voice didn't betray the nervous quiver I felt.

He inclined his head slightly, a gesture that seemed to acknowledge my presence without fully engaging. "Likewise," he replied, his voice smooth but distant.

I watched as he moved away, his stride confident and purposeful. It was clear he was a man accustomed to getting what he wanted, and the way he interacted with everyone around him suggested he had a clear vision of how things should be done. I couldn't afford to let any missteps or misjudgments on my part jeopardize this opportunity.

As the team prepared for the first shoot, I found myself getting caught up in the whirl of activity. Lighting was adjusted, props were positioned, and a flurry of last-minute decisions were made. I was introduced to various members of the crew, their names and faces blurring together in my anxious state.

I took a deep breath and made my way to the set, where Liam was already in position. He was a vision of elegance and control, every bit the high-fashion icon I had seen in magazines. He exuded an effortless charm, yet there was something in his eyes—an edge that hinted at the struggle behind the polished surface.

I could tell this shoot was going to be a challenge. Liam seemed to glide through the poses with a practiced ease, but there was a hardness to his gaze, a level of scrutiny that felt almost palpable. It was as if he was assessing everything with a critical eye, and I knew that every click of my camera would be under that same intense scrutiny.

I took my place behind the lens, adjusting settings and framing each shot with a meticulousness that spoke of countless hours spent perfecting my craft. Despite the pressure, I tried to stay in the moment, focusing on capturing the essence of Liam without letting his formidable presence intimidate me.

As the day wore on, I could feel the strain of maintaining professionalism while navigating the complexities of Liam's personality. He was a master at projecting an image, but it seemed there was a disconnect between the man I was photographing and the persona he presented to the world. There were moments when his smile would flicker, and his eyes would reveal a flicker of something raw and unguarded. But those moments were fleeting, slipping away before I could grasp their meaning.

By the end of the day, I was exhausted, both mentally and physically. Liam's performance had been impeccable, but the tension between us lingered in the air like an unspoken challenge. I retreated to my room, seeking solace in the quiet, away from the relentless demands of the day. The view from my terrace was as breathtaking as ever, the setting sun casting a warm, golden light over the coast.

I sank into a chair, my mind racing with thoughts and uncertainties. I had anticipated the challenges of working with someone of Liam's caliber, but the reality was even more daunting than I had imagined. His aloof demeanor and the pressure to perform were weighing heavily on me.

Despite the difficulties, there was a part of me that couldn't ignore the spark of intrigue he had ignited. Liam Hudson was a puzzle, and as much as he seemed to push me away, there was an undeniable pull that kept me wanting to understand him better. I knew that if I wanted to make this shoot a success, I had to find a way to bridge the gap between his world and mine.

As I sat there, the sky darkening and the stars beginning to emerge, I couldn't help but wonder what the coming days would bring. This was just the beginning, and though the road ahead seemed fraught with obstacles, I was determined to face them head-on. The Amalfi Coast was more than just a backdrop; it was the stage for a journey that was both professional and profoundly personal. And no matter how difficult Liam Hudson proved to be, I was ready to embrace whatever challenges lay ahead.

# Chapter 2:

The air inside the villa felt cooler than outside, and the high ceilings amplified the sound of my footsteps as I followed Liam's retreating figure. I moved cautiously, as if treading on thin ice, trying to gauge the mood of the place now that he had arrived. The villa's interior was just as magnificent as its exterior—modern and luxurious, yet subtly infused with classic touches. It was the kind of place that seemed almost too perfect, as though it were designed to be the backdrop of a dream.

Liam had already disappeared down a corridor by the time I reached the main hall, so I took a moment to collect myself, drawing in a deep breath. I had imagined this moment countless times, visualizing the ideal first meeting. But the reality was starkly different. His aloofness was palpable, a barrier I'd have to work hard to break down. The challenge of working with someone so distant felt daunting, but I had to remind myself of the stakes. This was a once-in-a-lifetime opportunity, and I couldn't afford to be disheartened by a rocky start.

I took the rest of the afternoon to familiarize myself with the villa's various rooms and the best locations for our photos. The sprawling gardens, with their manicured hedges and blooming flowers, offered countless possibilities. I imagined the kind of shots I could capture, blending Liam's striking presence with the villa's natural beauty. As I worked, I couldn't help but wonder what kind of person Liam truly was beneath his meticulously maintained exterior.

Dinner was a quiet affair. The crew had gathered in the dining room, their conversations hushed as they waited for Liam to make an appearance. When he did, he was even more striking up close, but his demeanor remained unchanged. He took his seat with an air of detachment, responding to polite conversation with curt nods and brief answers. I tried to engage him in light conversation, but his responses were clipped, leaving little room for further dialogue. It was clear that I was dealing with a man who had little interest in social niceties.

As the evening wore on, I found myself contemplating the challenge ahead. Liam's aloofness was unsettling, but I was determined not to let it derail my plans. I had come here to do a job, and I needed to focus on that. The beauty of the villa, the grandeur of the setting—it was all secondary to the task at hand.

After dinner, I retreated to my room, feeling the weight of the day's interactions press down on me. The villa was quiet, save for the occasional murmur of the ocean below. I took a moment to unwind on the terrace, allowing myself to be enveloped by the calm of the night. The stars glittered above, their brilliance a stark contrast to the tension I felt. I needed to approach the coming days with a fresh perspective, to find a way to connect with Liam despite the initial barriers.

As I gazed out at the sea, I couldn't shake the feeling that there was more to Liam than the image he projected. His aloofness might have been a shield, a way to protect himself from the pressures and expectations that came with his fame. If I could just peel back the layers, perhaps I would find something real beneath the polished surface. But for now, all I could do was prepare for the shoot and hope that over time, the distance between us would close.

The first day of the shoot dawned bright and clear. I woke early, feeling a mix of excitement and apprehension. I reviewed my notes, double-checking every detail to ensure that nothing was left to chance. The villa was still bathed in the soft morning light when I arrived in the main hall, ready to start the day.

Liam appeared on time, his demeanor unchanged but his professionalism undeniable. He was punctual and precise, moving with a practiced ease that spoke of years in front of the camera. Despite his cold exterior, there was a sense of determination in him that was almost admirable. I found myself wondering what it would take to break through the wall he had built around himself.

We began the first set of shots, working through various poses and settings with a focus that bordered on intense. I tried my best to remain unobtrusive, adjusting my camera and lighting with quiet efficiency. Liam's gaze was as sharp as ever, but as the hours passed, I noticed the faintest hint of something—maybe fatigue or frustration—softening his features. It was a small crack, but it was there, and I held onto that glimmer of hope as I continued to work.

I found myself alone in the expansive dining room as the crew went about their preparations, their whispers a background hum to my thoughts. I couldn't shake the feeling that the atmosphere was charged with unspoken tension, a silent acknowledgment of the difficulty ahead. As I glanced around, I could see the others casting occasional glances toward the entrance, as if waiting for some sign that Liam might thaw or perhaps give a hint of the person behind the public persona.

Later that night, I wandered outside to the villa's terrace, hoping the fresh air would help clear my mind. The sky was a canvas of deep indigos and scattered stars, the Mediterranean Sea stretching out like a shimmering blanket of dark velvet. The serenity of the view was a stark contrast to the turmoil brewing inside me. I leaned against the railing, letting the cool breeze ruffle my hair, trying to focus on the beauty of the night instead of the unsettling encounter I had just experienced.

I replayed our brief exchange over and over in my mind, analyzing every word and gesture. What had I done to make the interaction so cold? Was it something about me, or was it just Liam's way of protecting himself from the world? I knew I had to remain professional, but the distance between us seemed like an insurmountable chasm.

The following morning, I woke with a resolve to tackle the day with a fresh perspective. The villa came alive with the sounds of preparation as the crew busied themselves with final adjustments. I reviewed my shot lists and made some last-minute tweaks, determined to capture the essence of this extraordinary setting, regardless of the challenges Liam might pose.

When Liam finally emerged, he was already in his work mode, his demeanor shifting seamlessly from the distant figure I had met the previous day to the focused professional. He moved with an effortless grace, his presence commanding attention as he prepared for the day's shoot. The contrast between his public persona and private demeanor was striking, and I couldn't help but wonder which side would prevail in the days to come.

The first few hours of the shoot were a test of patience and adaptability. Liam was precise and demanding, his focus entirely on achieving the perfect shot. He moved through each pose with a mechanical precision, and though he occasionally offered a critique or direction, his tone remained cool and impersonal. I worked diligently to capture his best angles, trying to find a way to connect with him through the lens, hoping that if I could just get a glimpse of his true self, it might ease the tension between us.

During a brief break, I caught him alone on the terrace, staring out at the sea. It was a rare moment of vulnerability, and I seized the opportunity to approach him with a tentative, "How's everything going so far?"

He turned to me, his expression unreadable behind the dark sunglasses. For a split second, I thought I saw a flicker of something softer, maybe even weariness. "It's going fine," he said, his voice less clipped than before. "Just a lot of work."

I nodded, searching for the right words to bridge the gap between us. "I know it's a demanding schedule. If there's anything you need, just let me know."

He glanced at me, his gaze meeting mine through the lens of his sunglasses. "I'll keep that in mind," he said, though the distance in his tone suggested he wasn't entirely convinced.

I walked away with a renewed sense of determination, feeling as though I had made a small but significant breakthrough. The road ahead was still uncertain, but I had to believe that with persistence and patience, I could find a way to connect with Liam and make this shoot a success. The villa's breathtaking beauty and the promise of what we could create together kept me motivated, even in the face of the formidable challenge that lay before me.

# Chapter 3:

The villa's vastness seemed to echo the growing chasm between us, and I found myself sinking deeper into the routine of work, using it as an anchor to navigate through Liam's icy demeanor. Each day followed the same rhythm: early mornings spent setting up, hours of photographing with meticulous precision, and the silence that followed when the cameras were off. The air felt thick with unspoken words, and the space around us seemed to contract, leaving little room for anything beyond the sterile formality of our interactions.

The Mediterranean sun was relentless, pouring its golden light across the villa and turning every room into a stage for our daily performance. Liam adapted effortlessly to the light, his movements fluid and graceful despite the heat. Yet, his eyes remained hidden behind those dark sunglasses, and even in moments of unguarded repose, he seemed unreachable. It was as if his whole life was a carefully curated gallery, with every glimpse we caught being just a reflection of what he chose to show.

I tried to focus on the artistry of the shoot, pushing aside my frustrations and immersing myself in the beauty of the setting. The villa's terraces, with their panoramic views, became my sanctuary of sorts. There, with my camera in hand, I could lose myself in the interplay of light and shadow, the dance of color and form. And yet, every time I glanced over to where Liam stood, I was reminded of the emotional barricade that separated us. He was a model of perfection, but the perfection felt hollow without a sense of connection.

One afternoon, while adjusting the light for a particularly challenging shot, I found myself struggling with the equipment, my frustration building as I wrestled with the technicalities. Liam, ever observant, watched from a distance. His presence was like a shadow, always there but never quite tangible. He approached with the same quiet intensity that marked his demeanor throughout the shoot.

"Need some help?" His voice was calm, almost disarmingly so, cutting through the hum of the equipment.

I looked up, surprised by the offer. "If you don't mind. I'm having trouble with this setup."

He nodded, stepping closer and taking over the adjustments with a practiced ease that spoke of years of experience. As he worked, there was a brief moment when his focus seemed to shift from the equipment to me. The air between us crackled with something almost like understanding, but it was fleeting. His touch was gentle yet deliberate, and for a heartbeat, I felt a semblance of connection. But then, as quickly as it came, it was gone, replaced by his familiar, detached demeanor.

"Better?" he asked, his voice returning to its cool, professional tone.

"Yes, much better," I replied, trying to mask the disappointment I felt at the swift return to formality.

We continued the shoot, and the brief interaction lingered in my mind, a small crack in the armor he wore so meticulously. Yet, even with this rare glimpse, I found it hard to gauge if there was more beneath the surface or if it was simply a momentary lapse in his otherwise guarded persona. Each day seemed to reaffirm his need for distance, and I struggled to balance my growing curiosity with the professionalism I was determined to maintain.

As the week progressed, the routine became a monotonous dance of clicks and adjustments, with Liam's presence a constant reminder of the boundary that I couldn't cross. The villa, with its breathtaking vistas and serene atmosphere, felt like a cage of sorts—beautiful but confining. I poured my energy into the work, focusing on capturing the essence of the setting and Liam's impeccable performance, but the emotional disconnect was becoming harder to ignore.

In the quiet moments between shots, as I reviewed the images and prepared for the next round, I found myself grappling with the contrast between the public persona and the private individual. The challenge was not just in getting the perfect shot but in navigating the complexities of working with someone who seemed so intent on keeping everyone at arm's length. It was an unspoken battle, one that tested the limits of my patience and the depth of my resolve.

Despite the distance, I remained committed to my craft, driven by the hope that perhaps, in time, the barriers would begin to break down. The villa's beauty was undeniable, and every photograph I took was a testament to the artistic potential of the setting. Yet, beneath the surface of every image lay the unspoken tension, a reminder of the complex dance between professionalism and personal connection.

Our days settled into a predictable pattern. Mornings began with a crisp anticipation, a faint hope that maybe, just maybe, today might break the mold of our routine. But as soon as Liam appeared, any hope of warmth dissipated like morning mist under the harsh glare of the sun. His professional façade was consistent, a shield that never faltered. Each day, he slipped into his role with a seamless precision, every movement and pose executed with an almost mechanical perfection. It was clear he had mastered the art of being a model, but his mastery came with a price—an emotional detachment that made him an enigma I couldn't decipher.

Despite my best efforts to remain focused on the work at hand, there were moments when the silence between us felt oppressive. We'd been shooting in various locations around the villa—on the sun-drenched terraces, amidst the lush gardens, and in the opulent rooms that seemed to speak of old-world elegance. Each setting provided a new backdrop for Liam's poses, but no matter how beautiful the scenery or how expertly I framed each shot, there was always an underlying tension. The more I tried to engage him in conversation or to draw out a hint of genuine emotion, the more he retreated into his professional shell.

It was during one particularly hot afternoon, as the sun beat down mercilessly, that I found myself struggling with both the heat and my growing frustration. I had asked Liam to take a break, to grab some water and cool down. He had obliged with the same distant efficiency, retreating to a shaded corner while I fought with my camera settings.

I could feel his eyes on me, the weight of his gaze like a tangible presence. When I finally looked up, I caught him watching me with an intensity that was almost out of character. For a split second, there was something in his expression—a flicker of curiosity or maybe something softer. But before I could interpret it, he masked it with his usual impassive demeanor.

"You're determined," he said, his voice cutting through the ambient noise.

I met his gaze, trying to decipher the hint of something beneath his words. "I guess you could say that."

He nodded, almost imperceptibly. "It's good to see someone take their work seriously."

His comment was so dispassionate, so devoid of the warmth one might expect, that it left me with more questions than answers. But I couldn't afford to dwell on them. I had a job to do, and Liam was my responsibility. So I pushed aside my curiosity and focused on the task at hand.

The following days felt like a marathon of monotony. I immersed myself in the work, finding solace in the rhythm of the camera clicks and the gradual accumulation of perfect shots. Liam remained a stoic figure, his demeanor unchanging, and I began to resign myself to the fact that this was the way it was going to be. The photographs were beautiful, and the results spoke for themselves, but the process was devoid of any personal connection. I was documenting his image, not uncovering the person behind it.

One evening, as the golden light of the setting sun bathed the villa in a warm glow, Liam and I found ourselves alone on the terrace. The crew had finished for the day, leaving us with a quiet that felt almost intimate. I was packing up my equipment when Liam approached, his footsteps a soft echo on the stone floor.

"Nice work today," he said, his voice surprisingly gentle.

I looked up, momentarily taken aback by the change in tone. "Thanks. You made it easy."

He paused, studying me with an intensity that was rare. "You're not what I expected."

The statement hung in the air, ambiguous and open to interpretation. I didn't know how to respond, so I simply nodded, offering a polite smile.

Liam turned, his posture slightly more relaxed than usual. "Well, I guess we're stuck with each other for the next few weeks."

I watched him walk away, his silhouette merging with the fading light. For the first time, there was a sense that he might be more than just the distant figure I had come to know. But as always, he retreated into the shadows, leaving me with a renewed sense of curiosity and an ever-growing pile of questions about the man behind the image.

# Chapter 4:

The question hung between us, as tangible as the sea breeze that rustled around us. I could feel the weight of Liam's words, heavy with unspoken doubts and introspection. The serene beauty of the coastline seemed to amplify the rawness of the moment, making his vulnerability all the more striking.

I took a deep breath, feeling the warmth of the sun on my back as I tried to find the right words. "I think we all wonder about that sometimes," I began slowly. "The hustle, the constant push for more... It can be overwhelming. Sometimes, it makes you question if the sacrifices are worth the rewards."

Liam turned his head slightly, enough for me to catch a glimpse of his profile. His jaw was set, but there was a softness around his eyes that was new. He looked out at the sea again, as if searching for answers in the endless blue. "It's easy to get caught up in the glamour and the accolades," he said, his voice carrying a trace of weariness. "But when you're alone, away from the cameras and the flashing lights, it's hard not to wonder if it's all just a façade."

His admission startled me. It was as if I had peeled back a layer of armor he had meticulously crafted, exposing a part of him that was rarely seen. I had always imagined Liam as someone who thrived on the attention, who lived for the spotlight. To hear him speak so candidly about doubt and disillusionment was a revelation.

"Do you ever feel like you're just playing a part?" I asked, my curiosity getting the better of me. "Like the person everyone sees isn't really who you are?"

He didn't answer immediately, his gaze still fixed on the horizon. The silence stretched, filled only by the rhythmic crashing of waves against the rocks below. I watched him, noticing the subtle changes in his expression, the way his shoulders seemed to relax just a bit. It was a small victory, but it felt significant.

16

"Sometimes," he finally said, his voice barely above a whisper. "Sometimes, it feels like I'm just a character in a script someone else wrote. I'm not sure where the real me ends and the public persona begins."

The admission was raw, and it struck a chord deep within me. I had seen glimpses of this complexity in Liam, but hearing him articulate it so openly was something else entirely. It made me realize how much of his life was lived under a magnifying glass, how every gesture, every word, was scrutinized by a world eager to dissect his every move.

I wanted to say something comforting, to offer words that might ease the burden of his discontent. But the moment felt fragile, and I feared that any attempt at reassurance might come off as insincere. So, instead, I simply stood beside him, sharing the silence and the view.

For a while, we were both lost in our own thoughts, the sea providing a tranquil backdrop to our shared solitude. I could see the conflict in Liam's eyes, the struggle between his public success and private struggles. It was a look I hadn't expected to see, and it made me reconsider everything I thought I knew about him.

As the sun dipped lower in the sky, casting long shadows across the cliffs, Liam finally turned to me. "Thanks for... listening," he said, his voice softer than before. There was a note of gratitude in his tone, a subtle acknowledgment that this moment of honesty meant something to him.

I gave him a small smile, trying to convey my support without overstepping the boundaries of our professional relationship. "Anytime," I said simply. "If you ever need to talk or just need a break from the chaos, I'm here."

With that, the moment seemed to pass, and Liam's usual demeanor began to reassert itself. The distance returned, but it was less daunting now. I had seen a crack in his facade, and though it was just a small glimpse, it was enough to change how I viewed him.

As we headed back to the villa, the sun's last rays painting the sky in hues of pink and orange, I couldn't shake the feeling that things had shifted. The professional barriers that had once felt so solid now seemed a little less impenetrable. I was beginning to understand that behind the polished exterior, there was a man struggling with his own demons, and that knowledge was both sobering and oddly comforting.

The silence between us grew as I processed Liam's confession. His gaze remained locked on the horizon, his profile etched with a contemplative sorrow that was both captivating and disarming. I could sense the weight of his words, their significance resonating in the space that separated us. It was a rare glimpse into a part of him that was usually hidden behind the polished veneer of his public persona.

"Do you ever feel like you're living someone else's life?" I asked, feeling a surprising kinship with his doubts. "Like you're just playing a role and not really being yourself?"

Liam's head turned slightly, and for the first time, I saw a hint of something more genuine in his eyes. There was a flicker of vulnerability, a shadow of introspection that made him seem more human, less like the distant figure I had encountered in the beginning. He looked at me, and for a moment, the world seemed to shrink to just the two of us and the vast, open sea before us.

"I think about it all the time," he said quietly. "It's like I'm trapped in this elaborate charade, and the real me is buried somewhere beneath all the expectations and the glitz."

There was something profoundly intimate about the way he spoke, a raw honesty that cut through the layers of pretense he had maintained. It was as if, in that brief moment, he had allowed himself to be seen for who he truly was, stripped of the celebrity façade that had always been his shield.

"It's not just the work, is it?" I ventured, sensing that there was more to his struggle than just the pressures of his career. "It's the constant performance, the expectation to always be on. It must be exhausting."

Liam nodded, his expression reflecting a weariness that was almost palpable. "It is. And sometimes, I wonder if people ever really see me for who I am. Or if they're just enamored with the image I project."

I could empathize with his sense of isolation, the feeling of being seen only for what others wanted to see rather than for his true self. The intensity of the moment, combined with the serenity of the setting sun, created a delicate balance between our conversation and the quiet of the evening. The sun dipped lower, casting a warm, golden hue over the sea and the cliff, adding a layer of beauty to our shared moment of vulnerability.

"Do you think you'll ever find a way to balance the two?" I asked, wondering if there was a path forward for him, a way to reconcile the public persona with the private self.

He sighed, a sound that seemed to carry the weight of his inner turmoil. "I don't know. Sometimes I think it's impossible to truly balance them. But maybe it's about finding moments like this, where I can be honest and real, even if only for a little while."

There was a profound sadness in his words, but also a glimmer of hope—a realization that even within the constraints of his public life, there were moments of authenticity to be found. I could see it in the way he spoke, in the way his eyes held mine with a mixture of gratitude and relief.

"I'm glad you shared this with me," I said softly. "It's moments like these that make me see beyond the surface, to understand that there's more to you than just the model everyone knows."

Liam gave a small, appreciative nod. "Thank you for listening. It's not something I usually talk about."

As we stood there, watching the last light of day fade into twilight, I felt a new sense of connection between us. The barriers that had once seemed insurmountable were beginning to show signs of wear, and in their place, there was a fragile but genuine bond forming. It was as if the real Liam, the one behind the façade, was slowly emerging, and I was being allowed to see him, not just as a subject of my photographs but as a person.

The sun set completely, leaving us in the soft embrace of dusk. The sea continued its rhythmic dance against the cliffs, a reminder of the world beyond our shared moment. As Liam turned to head back to the villa, I followed, feeling a renewed sense of purpose and a deeper understanding of the man I was working with.

# Chapter 5:

The days continued their relentless march, each one melding into the next with a rhythm that was both familiar and increasingly intimate. Liam's presence was a constant, but the nature of his presence was shifting. The intensity of our interactions was palpable, charged with a tension that seemed to crackle in the air whenever we were near each other.

One afternoon, while we were setting up for a shoot in one of the villa's opulent rooms, I caught him watching me again. His gaze was more than just a glance—it was an intense, almost searching look that made my heart flutter unexpectedly. I was adjusting the light, trying to get the perfect angle, when I felt his eyes on me. I turned to find him standing not far away, his expression inscrutable yet filled with an emotion I couldn't quite identify. I cleared my throat and forced a professional smile, hoping to dispel the awkwardness that was starting to weave itself into our interactions.

"Need any help?" he asked, his voice softer than usual. It was a small gesture, but it felt significant, like a bridge being tentatively extended between us.

"No, I'm good," I replied, my voice betraying a hint of uncertainty. I could feel the heat rising in my cheeks, a physical reaction I wasn't entirely prepared for. "I think I've got it under control."

He nodded, but didn't move away. Instead, he stayed close, his presence a comforting weight that seemed to draw me in despite my best efforts to remain detached. The air between us felt charged, and the brief moments of silence that followed were filled with unspoken words and emotions that neither of us dared to voice.

As the week wore on, our interactions became increasingly charged with unspoken understanding. There were lingering touches as we passed each other, and moments when his eyes would meet mine with a warmth that was both thrilling and disconcerting. I began to notice the subtle ways he would try to engage with me—an offhand comment here, a shared laugh there. Each instance seemed to peel back another layer of the formal barrier we had maintained.

One evening, after a particularly long day, I was sitting alone on the terrace, trying to unwind with a glass of wine. The sun had dipped below the horizon, leaving the sky in deep hues of twilight. The villa was quiet, save for the distant murmur of the waves below. I was lost in thought when I heard the soft crunch of footsteps on the gravel behind me. I turned to see Liam approaching, a hesitant smile on his lips.

"Mind if I join you?" he asked, his voice gentle. There was an earnestness in his tone that was new, a departure from his usual aloofness.

I gestured to the empty space beside me, trying to ignore the quickening of my pulse. "Of course, please."

He settled down next to me, his proximity sending a shiver down my spine. For a while, we sat in comfortable silence, each of us lost in our own thoughts. The peacefulness of the evening, coupled with the close proximity of Liam, created a sense of intimacy that was hard to ignore.

"It's beautiful here," he finally said, breaking the silence. "I didn't really appreciate it at first. Too focused on the work, I guess."

I turned to look at him, surprised by the softness in his voice. "Sometimes it's easy to get caught up in the grind and forget to take a step back."

He glanced at me, a small smile playing at the corners of his mouth. "You always have a way of putting things into perspective."

There was something about his words, the way he looked at me, that made me feel seen in a way I hadn't expected. The connection between us, which had begun as a mere flicker of tension, now felt like a full-blown flame, warming and illuminating everything in its path.

The night grew darker, the stars beginning to shine above us. Liam's hand brushed against mine, a fleeting touch that sent a jolt of electricity through me. I locked down at our intertwined fingers, the gesture feeling both innocent and incredibly intimate. The line between professional and personal was blurring, and despite my best efforts to maintain my focus on the job, I found myself increasingly drawn to him.

As we continued to talk, the conversation flowing easily between us, I couldn't shake the feeling that something significant was happening. The barriers that had once defined our relationship were dissolving, revealing a connection that was both unexpected and profound. It was clear that whatever was brewing between us was more than just a fleeting attraction—it was becoming something much deeper, something that I wasn't sure how to navigate.

And so, as the evening wore on, with the stars twinkling above and the gentle sea breeze rustling around us, I couldn't help but wonder where this newfound closeness would lead. The stakes had never felt higher, and as much as I tried to keep my emotions in check, I knew that this was no longer just about the shoot. It was about us, and the growing attraction that was becoming impossible to ignore.

One evening, after a particularly long day, I found myself alone on the villa's terrace, seeking solace in the quiet that had settled over the Mediterranean. The sun had disappeared below the horizon, leaving behind a sky dotted with stars that twinkled like scattered diamonds. The distant hum of the ocean was a soothing backdrop, and I savored the solitude, hoping it would clear the confusion that had been swirling in my mind.

I was so lost in my thoughts that I didn't notice Liam approaching until he was almost upon me. He moved silently, his presence only announced by the soft rustle of the breeze against his clothes. I looked up to find him standing a few feet away, his gaze fixed on me with a level of intensity that made my breath catch.

"Mind if I join you?" he asked, his voice carrying a hint of hesitation that was out of character for him. He gestured toward the empty space beside me on the stone bench, his usual confidence replaced by a rare vulnerability.

"Not at all," I said, trying to keep my voice steady despite the way my heart was racing. I scooted over to make room, my mind racing through the possibilities of what this might mean.

He sat down beside me, close enough that I could feel the warmth emanating from him. For a moment, there was an uncomfortable silence, filled only by the distant crashing of waves and the gentle chirping of crickets. Liam seemed lost in his thoughts, his eyes on the darkening horizon.

"It's peaceful out here," he finally said, breaking the silence. His voice was softer than usual, almost reflective.

"It is," I agreed, trying to keep my tone casual even though every fiber of my being was attuned to the man sitting beside me. "Sometimes it's nice to just take a break from everything."

Liam turned his head to look at me, his gaze lingering on my face. There was something different in his eyes, something that suggested he was seeing me not just as the photographer but as someone he could actually talk to. "You know, I don't get a lot of moments like this," he said. "When everything just slows down and I can... think."

I looked at him, trying to decipher the emotions that flickered across his face. "I can understand that," I said. "It's easy to get caught up in the whirlwind of work and forget to take a step back."

He nodded, his eyes returning to the horizon. "I think that's why I've been... more distant lately. It's easier to keep people at arm's length, you know?"

The honesty in his words surprised me, and I found myself drawn to the idea of breaking through the barriers he had so carefully constructed. "Sometimes it's worth the risk to let people in," I said softly, hoping my words would resonate.

He turned to face me again, his expression softening. "Maybe. But it's not always easy to know who to trust."

The air between us seemed to crackle with an electric charge, a silent acknowledgment of the unspoken connection that had been growing. I could feel the warmth of his body next to mine, the subtle tension in his posture that hinted at a vulnerability he rarely showed. The distance that had once seemed insurmountable was now a thin veil, easily pierced by the intimacy of the moment.

Liam's hand brushed against mine as he shifted, and the touch sent a jolt through me. It was a fleeting contact, but it was enough to make my heart race. I glanced at him, meeting his gaze once more. There was a question in his eyes, an unspoken plea that mirrored the confusion I felt inside.

For a long moment, we just sat there, the silence between us filled with a shared understanding that neither of us was willing to fully articulate. The stars above seemed to dim in comparison to the intensity of the emotions swirling around us. It was as if the entire universe was holding its breath, waiting for us to make a choice, to acknowledge the shift that had occurred.

Eventually, Liam cleared his throat, breaking the spell. "I should probably get some rest," he said, his voice steady once more. He stood up, his usual confidence returning as he offered me a small, genuine smile. "See you tomorrow, Ava."

I watched him walk away, my heart still racing from the brief, yet profound connection we had shared. The night air was cooler now, but it did nothing to cool the heat that lingered in my chest. Whatever was brewing between us, it was becoming harder to ignore, and I couldn't shake the feeling that the lines between professionalism and something deeper were blurring with each passing day.

The evening unfolded like a scene from one of those dreamlike films where reality blurs with possibility. After a day filled with the kind of breathtaking shots that could make anyone fall in love with the Amalfi Coast, the crew decided to unwind with drinks on the terrace. The sun had just dipped below the horizon, painting the sky in shades of amber and violet, and the air was thick with the promise of a lingering warmth.

I had never been one to indulge in these sorts of celebrations, preferring instead to retreat into my own quiet corner. But tonight, with the atmosphere so charged and the wine flowing freely, I found myself drawn into the collective exuberance of the crew. I sipped slowly, savoring the taste of the rich red wine, and allowed myself to be swept up in the moment. The laughter, the clinking of glasses, and the easy camaraderie of the evening were intoxicating in their own way.

Liam had been a quiet observer for most of the night, a glass of wine in hand but his demeanor reserved. He sat slightly apart from the rest of us, his gaze occasionally drifting over the terrace as though he was lost in thought. The others, in various states of relaxation, eventually made their way to their rooms, leaving the villa in a hushed calm that seemed to heighten the sense of anticipation in the air.

It was in this quiet that Liam made his move. He approached me with a deliberate slowness that made my pulse quicken. The soft light from the lanterns cast a golden glow over his features, making him appear even more striking than usual. He stopped just a few inches from where I sat, his gaze locked onto mine with an intensity that sent shivers down my spine.

"You surprise me, Ava," he said, his voice barely more than a whisper. The softness of his tone contrasted sharply with the edge of something almost wistful in his eyes.

My heart raced as I looked up at him, trying to decipher the layers behind his words. "Different how?" I managed to ask, the question slipping out before I could fully process the shift in our dynamic.

Liam's expression was inscrutable, a blend of something like amusement and contemplation. He didn't answer immediately, instead letting the question hang between us. The silence that followed was heavy, charged with the unspoken words and emotions that seemed to pulse just beneath the surface. I watched as his eyes flickered toward the darkened horizon, then back to me.

The weight of his gaze was almost too much to bear, and I found myself gripping the edge of my chair, trying to steady the trembling in my hands. There was something about the way he was looking at me that felt intimate, almost dangerously close. My mind raced, trying to find a response that wouldn't reveal just how much his presence affected me.

Without a word, Liam stood up. The movement was fluid, almost languid, as though he was extending a final, unspoken invitation. He turned toward the villa, his silhouette outlined against the soft glow of the lanterns, and then began walking away. The space he left behind seemed to pulse with a lingering tension, the kind that makes your breath catch and your thoughts scatter.

I remained seated, the warmth of the wine in my veins mixing with the electric thrill of our conversation. There were questions swirling in my mind, each one more insistent than the last. What had Liam meant by his comment? Why had he felt the need to tell me that I was different, and what had prompted him to leave without providing an answer?

The night stretched out before me, filled with the distant sounds of the ocean and the gentle rustling of leaves. I found myself staring into the darkness, my thoughts a tangled mess of curiosity and longing. The evening had started as a celebration, but it had transformed into something more profound, something that left me both exhilarated and unsettled.

I took a deep breath, trying to center myself amid the whirlwind of emotions. Liam's unexpected departure had left me with a sense of unfinished business, and I was acutely aware that whatever had shifted between us was far from resolved. The night was still young, and the possibilities seemed endless, like the vast expanse of stars that now blanketed the sky.

I resolved to clear my head and regain my composure before retiring for the night. As I stood and stretched, the cool breeze on my face provided a welcome contrast to the heat of the evening. With each step I took toward my room, I tried to shake off the lingering effects of Liam's words and his intense gaze. Yet, no matter how hard I tried, the sense of anticipation and the unanswered questions remained, a tantalizing reminder that the night had only just begun.

The silence that followed his enigmatic comment stretched out, heavy with unspoken thoughts. The warm night air seemed to press in around us, making the terrace feel like a secluded island in a vast ocean. Liam's gaze never wavered from mine, and I could feel the intensity of his scrutiny, like a spotlight aimed straight at my heart.

For a moment, I was frozen, caught between the intoxicating pull of the night and the inexplicable force of Liam's presence. He took a deep breath, and the sound was almost imperceptible against the backdrop of distant waves crashing against the cliffs. I could see his face clearly now, illuminated by the soft, flickering light of the lanterns. There was a vulnerability in his eyes that I hadn't seen before, a trace of uncertainty that contrasted sharply with the confident facade he usually wore.

"Liam, wait," I called out softly as he turned to leave. My voice trembled slightly, betraying the storm of emotions roiling within me. I wanted to understand, to peel back the layers that seemed to shield him from the world, but I was afraid of what I might find.

He paused at the edge of the terrace, his back still to me. The faint outline of his silhouette against the starry sky was almost serene, yet there was something profoundly restless about the way he stood, his shoulders tense and his posture rigid.

"Why do you think I'm different?" I pressed, my voice more insistent now. I felt a pang of frustration mixed with a surge of longing. I wanted to break through the barrier that had kept him so distant, to find out what lay beneath his guarded exterior.

Liam turned slowly, his expression unreadable. He walked back towards me with deliberate steps, his gaze intense and unyielding. He didn't sit back down, choosing instead to stand close enough that I could feel the heat of his body, the closeness of our shared space.

"Because," he began, his voice barely more than a murmur, "you're not like the others." There was something raw in his tone, a note of honesty that I hadn't expected. His words were simple, but the way he said them—his eyes searching mine with an earnestness that was almost startling—made them feel profound.

I swallowed, trying to process the weight of his confession. "Not like the others?" I echoed, my mind racing to grasp the meaning behind his words.

He nodded, his gaze dropping to the floor momentarily before meeting my eyes again. "Most people I meet have an agenda, a reason for being around me. They want something, or they're trying to gain something from being in my orbit. But you—" He paused, as if searching for the right words. "You're different. There's a sincerity to you that's... rare."

The air between us felt charged, electric with the undercurrent of his confession. I could feel my heart pounding in my chest, each beat resonating with the vulnerability he had just laid bare. For a moment, the world outside of the villa seemed to fade away, leaving just the two of us in this fragile bubble of connection.

"Liam," I said, my voice trembling slightly as I tried to process the depth of his revelation, "I didn't mean to... surprise you. I'm just here to do my job. I didn't expect..." My words faltered as I struggled to articulate the emotions swirling inside me.

He reached out, his hand brushing against mine with a touch that was both tentative and deliberate. The contact was brief, but it was enough to send a shiver through me. His eyes met mine again, and there was a softness there that was almost haunting.

"You didn't expect what?" he asked, his voice barely above a whisper. His proximity was intoxicating, the warmth of his body radiating towards me, making it hard to think clearly.

I took a deep breath, trying to steady myself. "I didn't expect to be drawn to you like this," I admitted, my voice low and trembling. "I didn't expect to see this side of you."

Liam's expression shifted, a flicker of something—relief, perhaps, or hope—crossing his face. He took a step closer, closing the gap between us. "Neither did I," he admitted, his voice almost a sigh.

For a moment, we stood there, suspended in a space where time seemed to slow down. The world outside the terrace continued its quiet dance, but inside this moment, it felt as though everything had changed.

The silence between us was a living thing, breathing and shifting with the weight of unspoken words. Liam's eyes remained locked on mine, their intensity like a magnetic pull drawing me closer. I could feel the warmth from the lanterns mingling with the cool evening breeze, creating a paradoxical comfort that both calmed and unsettled me.

After what felt like an eternity, Liam finally spoke, his voice low and almost reverent. "You have this way of being present," he said, a hint of wonder in his tone. "Most people are just... here. But you—" He paused, searching for the right words, his gaze softening as he looked at me. "You actually seem to see things. You notice things that others miss."

His words sent a shiver down my spine, the raw sincerity in his voice disarming me. I'd spent so much of my life trying to blend into the background, to go unnoticed, that hearing Liam's acknowledgment felt like a strange, exhilarating validation.

I took a small step closer, feeling the electric charge between us intensify. "I've always been the observer," I admitted, my voice barely more than a whisper. "It's how I make sense of things. I guess it's how I stay sane."

Liam's eyes flashed with something unreadable, a mix of curiosity and something deeper, more personal. He seemed to consider my words, his expression thoughtful as he took another step closer. "I can see that," he said quietly. "It's a gift, but also a burden, isn't it? To be so attuned to the world around you."

His observation struck a chord, resonating with my own experiences. It felt strangely intimate, sharing this understanding with someone who had seemed so detached just days ago. I nodded, feeling a connection form between us that was both thrilling and terrifying. "It is," I agreed. "Sometimes it feels like a curse. Seeing everything so clearly makes it harder to ignore the things you wish you could."

Liam studied me for a moment, his gaze lingering on my face as if he was trying to read every thought and emotion that flickered across it. "You're not like the others," he repeated, his voice now a gentle caress. "You actually care."

Before I could respond, he reached out, brushing a stray lock of hair from my face with a tenderness that made my heart skip a beat. His touch was fleeting, but it left a trail of warmth that lingered on my skin. I could see the conflict in his eyes, a battle between the person he presented to the world and the one he was revealing in this private moment.

I took a deep breath, my mind racing with questions, emotions, and the undeniable attraction that seemed to grow stronger with each passing second. "Liam," I said softly, struggling to find the right words. "What are we doing here?"

He looked away, his jaw tightening as he seemed to grapple with his own thoughts. "I don't know," he admitted finally, his voice almost a whisper. "I didn't expect this. I didn't expect you."

There was a vulnerability in his confession, an openness that felt like a rare gift. It was as if, in this isolated moment, he was allowing himself to be seen in a way he hadn't allowed anyone else. It was both exhilarating and frightening, knowing that I was seeing him more clearly than he perhaps saw himself.

As the night deepened, the sounds of the villa's inhabitants retreating to their rooms became distant echoes, leaving us alone with our shared silence. Liam's words hung between us, heavy with promise and uncertainty. I wanted to reach out, to bridge the gap that still lay between us, but I also feared what might happen if I did.

Finally, he looked back at me, his expression softened by the moonlight. "Maybe we should just... see where this goes," he said, his voice a mix of hope and resignation. "No promises, no expectations."

I nodded, feeling a rush of emotions I couldn't quite name. There was something profoundly genuine in his offer, a willingness to explore the unknown that mirrored my own curiosity. "Okay," I said, my voice steady despite the whirlwind inside me. "Let's see where this goes."

As Liam turned to walk back into the villa, I felt a strange mixture of anticipation and apprehension. The night had opened a door, and as I followed him inside, I knew that nothing would be the same. The lines between professional and personal had blurred, and

I was stepping into uncharted territory, guided by the unexpected connection that had formed between us.

The next day, everything felt different. It was as if the villa, the very air around us, had been transformed overnight. The sun rose with a gentle warmth that seemed to wrap around the world in a new embrace, and the usually vibrant Mediterranean sky appeared even more brilliant, as if reflecting the subtle shift in the atmosphere.

Liam arrived at the shoot with a different energy. Gone was the distant, almost clinical aura that had surrounded him. He moved with a newfound ease, his poses flowing with a natural grace that seemed to come effortlessly. There was an almost palpable change in him, and it wasn't just in his body language. His gaze lingered on me in a way that felt charged, filled with an unspoken understanding that made my heart race. Each time our eyes met, there was a moment of silent connection, a shared memory of the night before that neither of us mentioned but both felt profoundly.

As I worked, adjusting lighting and shifting angles, I could sense Liam's presence beside me, not as a demanding figure, but as a quiet observer. His attention was no longer critical but appreciative, and it made the task of capturing his image both exhilarating and nerve-wracking. Every click of the shutter felt different, imbued with a new layer of meaning. Where before I had felt the pressure of his scrutiny, now I felt a strange blend of admiration and support that was both thrilling and unnerving.

Our interactions were minimal but laden with meaning. When I brushed past him to adjust a set piece or moved closer to get a better angle, there was an electric charge in the air. His fingers would occasionally graze mine, deliberately or not, and each touch felt like a spark igniting something deeper within me. I caught him watching me more than once, his gaze soft and contemplative, and every time, it made my pulse quicken.

During a brief break, I found myself alone with Liam on the terrace, the same place where our conversation had turned so intimate the night before. The sun was high in the sky, casting a warm glow over everything. Liam leaned against the railing, his gaze fixed on the distant horizon, lost in thought. I hesitated for a moment, unsure if I should approach him or give him space.

Eventually, I walked over, unable to ignore the magnetic pull between us. "You seem lost in thought," I said softly, trying to keep my voice light and casual.

He turned to me, a small, enigmatic smile playing on his lips. "Just thinking," he replied, his voice carrying a note of vulnerability that surprised me. "About how things change."

"Yeah," I said, feeling the weight of the unspoken words between us. "Things do change."

There was a brief pause, and for a moment, I wondered if he would say more, if he would acknowledge the shift between us. But he only nodded, a look of contemplation in his eyes. "It's strange, isn't it?" he said eventually. "How something can feel so certain one day and completely different the next."

I nodded, understanding all too well. "It's like everything becomes clearer, yet more complicated at the same time."

He looked at me, his gaze intense and searching. "Exactly. It's like the more you understand, the more you realize you don't know."

His words resonated deeply, and I found myself drawn closer to him, both emotionally and physically. The space between us felt charged, filled with a new kind of tension that was different from before. It was as if the barriers we had built up were starting to crumble, revealing something more vulnerable and raw underneath.

The rest of the day passed in a haze of heightened awareness. Liam's presence seemed to fill the room with a new energy, and every interaction between us carried a weight that was impossible to ignore. The professional distance that had once felt so comfortable now felt like a thin veneer, barely concealing the deeper emotions that were beginning to surface.

As the day drew to a close, I couldn't shake the feeling that everything had shifted. The familiarity of our earlier interactions had been replaced by something more intense, something that left me both excited and apprehensive. The villa, with its stunning views and warm ambiance, seemed to echo the changes within me. Each sunset now felt like a reminder of the unspoken connection between Liam and me, a connection that was growing stronger with each passing moment.

Liam's gaze, once so cold and distant, had become a source of fascination and unease. The unspoken understanding between us was both a comfort and a source of tension, and I couldn't help but wonder what the future held. The line between professional and personal had blurred, and with each passing day, it became harder to maintain the distance I had once relied on.

Our new dynamic was both exhilarating and disconcerting. As the days wore on, the unspoken connection between us seemed to deepen, threading through every interaction, every moment spent in each other's orbit. Liam's usual rigidity was replaced by an openness that was almost unsettling. During breaks, he would engage in light conversation, his words laced with a casual intimacy that was new for us. The way he looked at me, with that soft intensity, made me question everything I thought I knew about him.

It was one afternoon, amidst the backdrop of sunlit terraces and the distant hum of the sea, that I felt the shift most acutely. We were between shots, and Liam had retreated to a quiet corner of the villa's garden, where the flowers bloomed in a riot of colors. I was adjusting the setup for the next scene when I noticed him there, resting against a stone wall, lost in thought.

His profile was bathed in the golden light of the setting sun, and he looked almost serene. The sight of him so vulnerable and unguarded made something inside me flutter. I wanted to approach him, to bridge the gap that had silently grown between us, but something held me back. I was afraid of what might happen if I crossed that invisible line.

Yet, the pull was undeniable. I found myself gravitating towards him, unable to ignore the magnetic force that seemed to draw us together. "Hey," I said softly as I reached him, careful to keep my voice light and unassuming. Liam turned his head slowly, his eyes meeting mine with an expression that was both curious and inviting.

"Hey," he replied, his voice carrying a warmth that was new and unfamiliar. For a moment, we stood there in silence, the air between us charged with unspoken words. It felt as though the world had narrowed to just the two of us, the bustling activity of the shoot fading into the background.

"I've been thinking," Liam began, breaking the silence with a hesitant smile. "About what you said the other night. About being different." His gaze was steady, his eyes reflecting the soft hues of the sunset. "I think you're right. You are different." The admission was unexpected, and it made my heart skip a beat.

Before I could respond, he continued, "You've managed to see something in me that I haven't shown anyone in a long time. It's... refreshing." His words were honest, and they carried a weight that felt heavy and significant. I could sense that he was offering a glimpse into a part of himself he rarely revealed, and it made me want to know more.

"I didn't mean to," I said, my voice barely above a whisper. "I was just trying to do my job." But even as I spoke, I knew that wasn't entirely true. Something about Liam had drawn me in, had made me want to peel away the layers of his guarded exterior to see the person beneath.

Liam took a step closer, his proximity sending a shiver down my spine. "You did more than just your job," he said softly. "You made me feel something I'd almost forgotten. And I don't know what to do with that." His confession was raw and honest, and it made my heart ache in the most beautiful way.

I swallowed hard, trying to steady the emotions that were swirling within me. "I don't know what to do with it either," I admitted. "But I do know that whatever this is—this shift between us—it's real. And it's more complicated than I ever expected."

His eyes searched mine, as if looking for answers that neither of us had. The silence that followed was thick with the weight of our shared understanding, and it was clear that neither of us was willing to break it. Liam's presence was overwhelming in its intensity, and I found myself drawn to him in a way that defied logic.

Finally, Liam spoke again, his voice barely more than a whisper. "Maybe we're both trying to figure out what this means. But for now, can we just... be? No expectations, no pressure?" The plea in his voice was sincere, and it resonated with a vulnerability that made my heart ache with a mixture of fear and longing.

I nodded, feeling a sense of relief mixed with trepidation. "Yeah, let's just be." The agreement was a fragile promise, a tentative step into the unknown, but it was all we had for now.

As the sun continued to set, casting a warm, golden glow over everything, Liam and I stood together in the garden, the air around us charged with an unspoken promise. The shift between us was undeniable, and though it scared me, it also held a strange allure. Whatever lay ahead, I knew that this moment, this connection, was a turning point. And as we stood there, side by side, I couldn't help but wonder where this new path would lead us.

He looked at me with a mixture of vulnerability and something else—something deeper, more profound. His voice softened even more, becoming almost a whisper as he said, "I think you're different in the best possible way. You're... real, Ava. More real than anyone

I've met in a long time." The sincerity in his words wrapped around me like a warm embrace, leaving me momentarily breathless.

The garden around us seemed to hold its breath, the vibrant colors of the flowers now just a backdrop to the intimate moment we were sharing. I wanted to respond, to tell him how his words had struck a chord deep within me, but the words felt inadequate. Instead, I took a step closer, drawn by an invisible thread that seemed to bind us together.

For a brief, electrifying moment, our eyes locked, and I felt as though we were alone in our own world, separated from everything else. The air between us crackled with a tension that was both exhilarating and frightening. I could see the way Liam's gaze softened, how he looked at me not just as a model but as a person—a person who had managed to crack through the facade he wore so well.

As if sensing the depth of the moment, Liam took a deep breath and ran a hand through his hair, a gesture that seemed both nervous and introspective. "I'm sorry if I've been... difficult," he said, his voice barely above a murmur. "It's just... I don't know how to let people in. Not anymore." His admission was a raw, unfiltered glimpse into the man behind the carefully constructed mask.

My heart ached at his words. I wanted to reach out, to bridge the gap that had kept us apart for so long. "You don't have to be sorry," I replied softly. "I get it. It's not always easy to open up, especially when you've been hurt before."

He nodded, his eyes reflecting the golden hues of the setting sun. "You make it seem easy, though," he said, his tone carrying a trace of admiration. "You're not afraid to show who you are, and it's... refreshing."

The sincerity in his voice made me feel exposed, vulnerable, and yet I couldn't deny the connection I felt with him. It was as if, in that quiet garden, we were shedding the layers of pretense that had kept us at a distance. I took a deep breath, trying to steady the whirlwind of emotions that was stirring inside me.

"I'm not sure I'm as brave as you think," I confessed, my voice trembling slightly. "Sometimes, I'm just as scared as you are. But maybe that's why we understand each other."

Liam's gaze softened even further, and he took a step closer, his proximity sending a shiver down my spine. "Maybe," he said quietly, his voice almost a caress. "Or maybe it's because we're both searching for something real in a world that's anything but."

The weight of his words hung in the air between us, and I felt a sudden, overwhelming urge to close the distance. But just as I took a tentative step forward, the sound of footsteps and laughter approached from the direction of the villa. The spell was broken, and reality rushed back in with its demands and distractions.

Liam straightened up, his expression becoming more guarded again, as if he was pulling himself back into the shell he had carefully constructed. "We should get back," he said, his tone shifting to its familiar professional edge. "The crew will be wondering where we are."

I nodded, feeling the sharp pang of disappointment as the moment slipped away. As we walked back towards the villa, the garden's tranquility was replaced by the bustling activity of the crew preparing for the next day. Yet, despite the return to normalcy, something fundamental had changed between us. The tension that had once felt oppressive now seemed to pulse with a new energy—an energy that neither of us could ignore, even as we tried to pretend it didn't exist.

The evening's conversation lingered in my mind as I made my way to my room. The way Liam had opened up, even if just a crack in his armor, had shifted something deep inside me. I found myself hoping that this newfound connection would evolve into something more meaningful, even as I grappled with the uncertainty of what that might mean for both of us.

As the days slipped by, the dynamic between Liam and me continued to evolve. It was like a delicate dance, each step revealing more of the person behind the public persona. The more I got to know him, the more I found myself drawn to the complexity of his character.

The shoot had a new rhythm now. Liam's once-perfunctory poses were imbued with a newfound authenticity. There was a fluidity in his movements that mirrored the ease he was starting to show off-camera. During breaks, he lingered around, no longer retreating to the corners or checking his phone with the usual frequency. Instead, he'd sidle up to where I was, watching me adjust my camera settings or review the shots we'd taken.

He began to ask questions about my work, about the stories behind the photographs I'd captured. It was strange, this shift from him being the subject of my lens to showing genuine interest in the craft itself. "What inspired you to choose photography?" he asked one afternoon, leaning against a wall with a casual ease that made my pulse quicken. His eyes were earnest, reflecting a curiosity that seemed far removed from the distant demeanor he'd initially shown.

I found myself opening up, sharing fragments of my life that I usually kept guarded. I told him about the first time I'd picked up a camera, about how the click of the shutter had felt like a revelation. I spoke of my dreams, my hopes to capture moments that told stories beyond words. There was a connection in these exchanges, something that felt both thrilling and intimate.

In return, Liam began to peel back the layers of his own life. It started with small anecdotes—an awkward audition, a humorous mishap on set. But soon, his stories turned more personal. One evening, as we sat together on the villa's terrace, the golden light of the sunset casting long shadows, he shared something more profound.

"It's not as glamorous as people think," he said, his voice soft, almost lost in the rustle of the wind. There was a heaviness in his tone that spoke volumes, more than the words alone could convey. "Everyone sees the red carpets, the photoshoots, the fame, but they don't see the isolation. The constant scrutiny. The pressure to be perfect all the time." His gaze was distant, his eyes reflecting a sadness I hadn't expected.

I listened, my heart aching at the vulnerability he was showing. It was like watching the walls he'd built around himself slowly crumble. "I imagine it's hard," I said quietly, reaching out to touch his hand. "I can't imagine living under that kind of spotlight."

He looked at me, his eyes meeting mine with a mixture of gratitude and something softer—an emotion I couldn't quite name. "It is," he admitted, his voice barely a whisper. "But talking to you... it's different. You make me feel like I can be myself, even if just for a little while."

There was a raw honesty in his words that made my heart race. I felt a sudden, fierce protectiveness for him, an urge to shield him from the world's harshness. "I'm glad you feel that way," I said, squeezing his hand gently. "I'd like to think that I can make things a bit easier, even if only for a short time."

The warmth of his hand against mine was a stark contrast to the chill of the evening air. We sat in companionable silence for a few moments, the stars beginning to twinkle above us. It was as if we were cocooned in our own private world, separate from the constraints of his fame and the demands of my work.

In the days that followed, our interactions continued to be punctuated by these moments of genuine connection. Liam's demeanor became less guarded, his conversations more open. I discovered more about the man behind the public image—the person who struggled with the pressures of fame, who found solace in simple moments of honesty.

I found myself looking forward to these moments, to the way he would smile when he talked about something he loved or how his eyes would light up when he shared a personal anecdote. It was as though every shared story, every honest exchange, was a brick removed from the wall he had built around himself.

And with each day, I couldn't help but feel that the lines between our professional relationship and something more personal were blurring. It was both exhilarating and terrifying, this new dynamic between us. I knew that whatever was growing between us was fragile, but it was real. And it was starting to make me question everything I had once taken for granted.

Liam's revelations were like cracks in a dam, letting streams of truth flow where before there had only been a rigid facade. I found myself captivated by these glimpses into a world I had only seen from the outside. As he shared more about the pressures of fame, the weight of constant public scrutiny, and the loneliness that accompanied his success, I couldn't help but feel a growing sense of empathy for him.

One late afternoon, as the sun dipped low on the horizon and painted the sky with hues of amber and rose, we found ourselves sitting side by side on the edge of the terrace. The villa's garden stretched out before us, a tranquil expanse that seemed to stand in stark contrast to the chaos of Liam's inner world.

"It's funny," he said, staring out at the sprawling landscape, "I used to think that fame was a ladder to happiness. But all it's done is put me in a glass box. People look at me and see what they want to see, not who I really am." His voice was barely a whisper, carried away by the evening breeze. There was a weariness in his tone, an exhaustion that spoke of more than just the demands of his career.

I wanted to reach out, to offer some kind of comfort, but words felt inadequate. Instead, I nodded, trying to convey my understanding through the quiet companionship of my presence. "It must be hard," I said softly, not knowing if it was enough, but feeling the need to acknowledge his struggle.

"It is," he admitted, turning his gaze towards me. His eyes, usually so guarded, were now open and vulnerable. "Sometimes I wonder if people would even like me if they knew the real me. The one who's not always smiling for the camera or pretending everything's perfect."

The weight of his words settled heavily between us. I realized how deeply lonely he must have felt, isolated by the very success that had seemed so enviable from the outside. For all his charisma and talent, he was still human, grappling with insecurities and fears just like anyone else.

As the conversation deepened, I found myself sharing more of my own life, my own dreams and fears. It was almost therapeutic, this exchange of personal truths. I spoke of the challenges I faced in my career, the moments of self-doubt, the relentless pursuit of capturing the perfect shot that often left me questioning my own worth.

In those moments, the divide between us seemed to dissolve. Liam, who had once been a distant figure shrouded in celebrity, was now someone I felt I could understand, someone whose struggles resonated with my own. The more we talked, the more the walls we had each erected began to crumble. It was as if the night itself was stripping away our defenses, leaving behind a raw, honest connection.

We talked long into the night, sharing stories and confessions beneath the blanket of stars. The villa, once a symbol of separation and isolation, now felt like a sanctuary where we could be ourselves. Liam's laughter, genuine and unguarded, was a revelation. It was a sound I hadn't heard before, one that spoke of a joy and relief he rarely allowed himself to feel.

As the conversation wound down and we sat in comfortable silence, I realized how much I had come to appreciate these moments with him. The attraction I felt towards Liam had shifted from a mere physical response to something far more profound. I was drawn to his vulnerability, his honesty, and the way he allowed me to see parts of him that were usually hidden behind the spotlight.

When the night finally settled into stillness, Liam stood, stretching with a relaxed grace that seemed to come from a place of genuine contentment. "Thanks for listening, Ava," he said quietly, a soft smile playing at his lips. "It means more than you know."

I smiled back, feeling a warmth in my chest that went beyond the fading embers of our conversation. "Anytime," I replied, my voice steady despite the whirlwind of emotions inside me. As he turned to go, I watched him disappear into the shadows of the villa, knowing that this shift in our relationship had opened doors to possibilities I hadn't anticipated.

The walls between us were down, and what lay ahead was uncertain but undeniably promising.

In those quiet moments, sitting side by side as the twilight wrapped the world in its soft embrace, the distance between us seemed to dissolve. Liam's presence was no longer a barrier to be navigated but a comfort, a sanctuary from the loneliness he had so candidly shared. As he spoke about the emptiness that sometimes haunted his fame, I saw the layers of his facade peeling away, revealing the man beneath the polished surface.

His revelations were both disarming and illuminating. He talked about the pressure to constantly perform, the expectations that weighed heavily on him like an unseen shroud. "People see the spotlight, but they don't see the shadows it casts," he said, his eyes reflecting the dimming light. The way he looked at me, as if searching for understanding, made my heart ache with a deep, unspoken empathy.

I found myself opening up more than I ever intended, sharing snippets of my own struggles and triumphs. My career in photography had its own set of challenges—unpredictable clients, the pressure to constantly innovate, and the fear of never being good enough. I spoke of the joy I found in capturing moments that told stories, how each photograph was a piece of myself, laid bare for the world to see.

"It's strange, isn't it?" I mused aloud. "How we both wear these masks to navigate our worlds. Yours is the charming, elusive star, and mine is the dedicated artist who hides behind the lens. But here, in these moments, we're just... people."

Liam's gaze softened as he listened, his expression a mixture of contemplation and gratitude. "Maybe that's why I feel this connection with you," he said quietly. "You see me for who I am, not who I'm supposed to be. It's rare, and it's... refreshing."

The sincerity in his voice made my pulse quicken. It was a confession wrapped in vulnerability, and it tugged at something deep within me. There was a growing intimacy between us, an unspoken understanding that transcended the professional boundaries we had maintained. I could feel the shift, the way our conversations had become more than just polite exchanges—they were becoming a dance of shared experiences and emotions.

As the night deepened, the villa's terrace grew cooler, the warmth of the sunset replaced by a crisp, comforting chill. Liam's proximity was both thrilling and unsettling. The space between us seemed to shrink with every word, every shared glance. He reached out, brushing a stray lock of hair from my face, his touch lingering for a moment longer than necessary.

"That's a beautiful way to put it," he said, his fingers still grazing my cheek. His touch was gentle, but it held a promise of something more. "I've never really had anyone see me like this before."

I swallowed, my breath hitching in my throat. "And I've never met anyone like you," I admitted, the words slipping out before I could fully grasp their weight. "You've shown me a side of you that I didn't expect, and I'm grateful for that."

His gaze held mine, intense and searching. "I think we both needed this," he said softly. "We needed to break down the walls we've built, to let someone in. For me, it's been a long time since I felt this... connected."

The moment was electric, charged with a tension that neither of us could ignore. The air between us was thick with unspoken possibilities, and the world outside seemed to fall away. It was as if time had stopped, leaving just the two of us in this fragile, poignant bubble.

As the evening wore on, the villa's lights flickered on, casting a warm glow over the terrace. The intimacy of our conversation had made the transition from daylight to night feel almost surreal, like a dream where nothing existed except the feelings we were exploring.

When we finally stood to leave, Liam's hand brushed mine, a fleeting touch that left me longing for more. His eyes met mine, and in that silent exchange, I felt a profound shift. The barriers we had carefully maintained were no longer there, replaced by an unspoken promise of something more.

"Thank you," he said quietly, his voice holding a note of sincerity. "For tonight."

I smiled, my heart full yet tinged with uncertainty. "You're welcome. For everything."

As we walked away from the terrace, the night sky stretching endlessly above us, I couldn't help but feel that this was just the beginning. The connection we had forged was fragile yet powerful, a thread woven between us that was both delicate and resilient. And as we continued to navigate the complexities of our lives, I knew that whatever lay ahead, we would face it together, with the walls we had once relied upon now broken down.

The villa was silent that night, the kind of silence that wraps around you and makes you acutely aware of every sound—the creak of the floorboards, the hum of the air conditioning. The crew had retired to their rooms, leaving Liam and me alone in the dim light of the studio. We were sifting through the photos from the day's shoot, the soft glow of the laptop screen casting a gentle illumination on our faces. His proximity was intoxicating, his presence so close that I could feel the warmth radiating from him, mingling with the cool night air.

Our shoulders brushed as we leaned in to examine the images, an unspoken closeness hanging heavily between us. I could smell the faint hint of his cologne, a scent that now seemed inseparable from the thrill of our recent conversations. It was in those moments, amid the blur of images and the quiet clicks of the laptop, that the boundaries we had so carefully maintained began to erode.

Liam's fingers brushed mine as he adjusted the settings on the camera, a seemingly innocent touch that sent a jolt through me. I glanced up, meeting his gaze, and in that instant, everything else fell away. There was a vulnerability in his eyes, an invitation that spoke louder than words. My pulse raced as I saw him—really saw him—in a way that went beyond the surface. All the walls we'd built, all the pretense of professionalism, seemed to dissolve in the electric air between us.

And then it happened. Without warning, without thought, I closed the distance between us and kissed him. It was a desperate, unrestrained collision of emotions, a moment where nothing else mattered but the feeling of his lips against mine. The kiss was raw, filled with all the longing and confusion that had been building up over the past weeks. It was as if the world outside had ceased to exist, leaving just the two of us suspended in a bubble of intimacy.

The taste of him was both thrilling and disorienting, a blend of passion and something deeply vulnerable. For a few precious seconds, everything felt right—so right that it was almost surreal. But just as quickly as the moment began, it shattered. Reality crashed back in like a wave, pulling me out of the dreamlike state I'd been lost in. I pulled away, my breath coming in short, uneven gasps.

Liam's expression mirrored my own turmoil. His eyes were wide, searching mine as if to find answers to questions neither of us were ready to confront. "We can't," I whispered, the words barely escaping my lips. I knew they were true, that crossing this line could jeopardize everything—the shoot, my career, the fragile connection we had built. Yet even as I spoke, doubt gnawed at me. The sincerity in his gaze, the way he had responded to the kiss, made it hard to convince myself that this was the end.

The silence that followed was heavy, laden with unspoken regrets and unvoiced desires. Liam's hand remained suspended in the air, as if reaching for something that had just slipped away. I could see the struggle in his eyes, the conflict between the professional façade he had worn and the raw honesty that had emerged between us. The kiss had been a breach, an unexpected crossing of boundaries that neither of us had planned but both felt deeply.

"Maybe we should talk about this," Liam said eventually, his voice rough with emotion. His words hung in the air, a suggestion of normalcy in the midst of the chaos we had just created. But I could feel the distance between us growing, the realization of what we had done pulling us apart.

"Yeah," I said, my voice barely a whisper. "Maybe we should." I turned away, needing space to process what had just happened. The weight of the kiss, the intensity of the moment, was too much to handle all at once. I needed to think, to find a way to make sense of the collision of our worlds and what it meant for the future.

Liam's presence remained in the room, a palpable reminder of the boundary we had crossed and the consequences that lay ahead. The air between us felt charged, and as I looked back at him, I saw the same uncertainty reflected in his eyes. We were standing on the precipice of something profound, something that could change everything, but neither of us knew how to navigate the aftermath of our impulsive, all-consuming kiss.

The silence in the studio was deafening after I pulled away from the kiss. The air seemed to grow colder, the vibrant energy of the moment replaced by a heavy, almost tangible tension. I stared at Liam, whose expression was a mix of surprise and something deeper, something that mirrored my own confusion. My breath came in uneven bursts as I tried to regain some semblance of control. The lingering warmth of his lips on mine was a stark contrast to the chill of my sudden realization.

"We can't," I whispered again, though this time my voice was tinged with uncertainty. I knew it was the right thing to say, the professional thing to say, but the words felt hollow, like an echo in a cavern. The kiss had been a mistake, an impulsive action that crossed boundaries I had worked so hard to maintain. But as I looked into his eyes, I saw a flicker of something that suggested he wasn't entirely convinced by my words.

Liam's gaze dropped to the floor, his jaw clenched as if he were wrestling with his own thoughts. He took a deep breath, trying to steady himself, and I watched as he struggled to reassemble the façade he had so carefully built. The intimacy we'd shared moments before was now replaced by an awkward distance, a chasm that seemed insurmountable. I felt a pang of regret, mixed with a confusing rush of emotions that I wasn't prepared to confront.

"I'm sorry," I said, my voice breaking slightly. The apology felt inadequate, almost insignificant in the face of what had just transpired. I wanted to reach out to him, to bridge the gap that had suddenly opened between us, but I was paralyzed by the fear of making things worse.

Liam finally looked up, his expression unreadable. He nodded, a gesture that seemed to convey acceptance, or perhaps resignation. "It's okay," he said, though his voice lacked conviction. "I didn't expect—" He stopped himself, shaking his head as if trying to clear the fog of his thoughts. "Forget it. Let's just... forget it."

His words stung more than I'd anticipated. The idea of erasing what had happened, pretending it was just a fleeting mistake, was both a relief and a profound disappointment. I nodded, trying to match his nonchalance, but inside, I was a whirlwind of conflicting emotions.

We returned to the task at hand, the photos on the laptop suddenly seeming insignificant in the face of the storm we had just weathered. The once-familiar comfort of our working relationship had been irrevocably altered, and the ease with which we had collaborated before now felt distant and strained. Each click of the mouse seemed louder than it had moments ago, each glance more laden with unspoken words.

The rest of the night passed in a haze of awkward silence. Liam worked quietly beside me, his movements mechanical, as if he were trying to bury his thoughts in the routine of the job. I could feel the weight of his presence beside me, an almost palpable reminder of the barrier that now existed between us. It was a stark contrast to the easy camaraderie we had shared only days before, and the change was both jarring and disheartening.

As we wrapped up for the night, the tension between us remained unresolved, hanging in the air like a specter. I felt a deep sense of loss, a recognition that something had shifted in our dynamic, something that might never be the same. The professional boundaries we had carefully navigated seemed now to be entangled with a complex web of personal emotions, and I was left grappling with the aftermath of our impulsive crossing of the line.

Liam gave a terse nod as he left the studio, his face a mask of composure that didn't quite reach his eyes. I watched him go, my heart heavy with the knowledge that whatever had been between us was now a fragile, uncertain thing. The night had changed everything, and as I turned off the lights and closed the studio door behind me, I couldn't shake the feeling that the real consequences of our actions were yet to come.

Liam's eyes held mine for a moment longer, as if he were searching for a trace of something that might validate the kiss we'd just shared. But as the silence stretched, the weight of our choices settled heavily between us. His face softened, and for a fleeting second, I saw vulnerability there—something raw and unguarded that contrasted sharply with the confident mask he wore in public.

I tried to pull myself together, to focus on the task at hand, but my hands trembled as I fumbled with the camera. Liam moved to the other side of the room, distancing himself from me both physically and emotionally. The shift was palpable, like a cold breeze that swept through the room, leaving an unsettling chill in its wake. I could feel my heart beating erratically, a relentless reminder of the intimacy that had just occurred.

"Maybe we should get some rest," I suggested, my voice lacking the usual firmness. I didn't know how to bridge the gap that had suddenly appeared between us, how to fix the jagged edges of the moment we had just shared. The idea of retreating to our separate spaces seemed like the only logical choice, but it did little to soothe the turmoil inside me.

Liam nodded in agreement, his gaze drifting away as if he were lost in thought. "Yeah," he said quietly. "Maybe that's a good idea."

We parted ways without another word, the unspoken understanding hanging heavily in the air. As I made my way to my room, the echo of the kiss reverberated through my mind. Each step felt heavier than the last, the reality of what had happened settling around me like a shroud. The walls I had so carefully constructed to keep my emotions in check had been breached, and the aftermath was a tangled mess of regret and desire.

Lying in bed, I stared at the ceiling, unable to silence the whirlwind of thoughts racing through my head. The kiss had been a moment of weakness, of longing that had breached the boundaries I had set. But it had also been a revelation, a glimpse into something deeper and more complicated than I had anticipated. The fear of what it meant, of how it would change everything, gnawed at me.

I wondered about Liam, about his feelings and thoughts. Did he regret the kiss, or was he grappling with the same confusion and desire that plagued me? The thought of him alone in his room, wrestling with his own demons, made my heart ache. The connection we had shared, however fleeting, had revealed a side of him that was both unexpected and disarming. It was as if the walls he had built around himself had started to crumble, and in their place, something genuine and tender had emerged.

But the reality of our situation was inescapable. We were bound by the constraints of professionalism, by the intricate web of expectations and responsibilities that came with our roles. The kiss had crossed a line, and the consequences of that breach were yet to be fully understood. The potential fallout was daunting, and the weight of it pressed heavily on my chest.

As sleep eluded me, I couldn't shake the feeling that things would never be the same between us. The dynamics of our relationship had shifted, and the once-clear boundaries had become blurred and uncertain. The kiss had opened a door to possibilities I hadn't considered, and now I was left to navigate the complexities that lay beyond.

The morning light brought little comfort. The routine of the day felt mechanical, each task a reminder of the night before. Liam and I exchanged brief, polite nods, but the underlying tension was palpable. The shared secret of our kiss hung between us, an invisible thread that connected us in a way that was both intimate and isolating.

As we continued with the shoot, I focused on the work, trying to bury my emotions beneath layers of professionalism. But every glance, every accidental brush of our fingers, seemed to remind me of what had transpired. The pressure to maintain a facade of normalcy was immense, but the reality of our interaction was always lurking just beneath the surface.

The kiss had been a moment of profound clarity, a glimpse into a world where our boundaries were not so clearly defined. It was a reminder that beneath the surface of our carefully constructed lives, there was something real and raw that refused to be ignored. And as I worked alongside Liam, I knew that whatever lay ahead, the impact of that night would shape our future in ways neither of us could fully anticipate.

The morning after the kiss, a cloud of unspoken words hung heavily between Liam and me. It was as if an invisible barrier had been erected, separating us despite the physical closeness of the set. We moved through the motions of the day, each interaction laced with an uncomfortable formality that hadn't been there before. The usual ease of our exchanges had dissolved into a tense dance of avoidance and awkward glances.

The crew, ever perceptive, seemed to sense the shift. Whispers filled the air, though no one addressed the elephant in the room directly. I could feel their curiosity simmering just beneath the surface, and their avoidance only served to heighten the strain between Liam and me. Every time our paths crossed, the space seemed to narrow, leaving us with nothing but the weight of our shared silence.

As I set up my equipment, my thoughts were consumed by fragments of the night before—the feel of his lips on mine, the electricity of the moment that had felt both exhilarating and terrifying. My hands moved mechanically, adjusting the camera settings without truly seeing them. The kiss had been a stark departure from the professional boundaries I had so meticulously maintained, and the ramifications of that breach were beginning to sink in.

Liam's demeanor was equally distant, his interactions terse and his focus scattered. When he spoke to me, it was with a formality that bordered on coldness, as if he were trying to erase the intimacy that had existed between us. I could see the effort he was putting into maintaining this distance, but it only served to deepen the rift between us.

During a brief break, I found myself alone, seated on a low wall overlooking the picturesque landscape. The view was beautiful, but it offered little solace. My mind was a tumultuous sea of emotions, and I couldn't shake the feeling that everything had irrevocably changed. I wondered if Liam felt the same way—if the kiss had affected him as profoundly as it had me.

The crew began to gather for the next round of shots, their chatter a distant murmur in the background. I took a deep breath, trying to steady my nerves and focus on the task at hand. But no matter how hard I tried, my thoughts kept drifting back to Liam and the uncertainty that now defined our relationship.

When Liam approached, his presence was like a gust of wind, stirring up the tension that had settled around us. He offered a polite nod, his eyes avoiding mine. I could sense the inner conflict within him, the struggle to maintain a professional facade while grappling with the emotional fallout of our kiss.

The rest of the day passed in a blur of activity and forced interactions. The cameras clicked, lights flashed, and directions were given, but all the while, my heart was tethered to the unresolved tension between Liam and me. Each shared glance, each brush of our hands, seemed to carry a weight of unspoken regret and longing.

As the day drew to a close, I was exhausted, both physically and emotionally. The crew packed up, and the villa slowly emptied of its vibrant energy, leaving behind an echo of what had been. I tried to find a moment of solitude, but Liam's presence was a constant reminder of the boundaries we had crossed and the questions that now loomed.

The evening brought no relief, as the night seemed to stretch endlessly before me. I replayed the day's interactions in my mind, searching for answers that remained frustratingly out of reach. The kiss had changed everything, but the path forward was unclear. The line we had crossed was a chasm, and I was left to navigate the fallout of our actions.

As I prepared for bed, I glanced out the window at the moonlit landscape, a serene contrast to the turmoil inside me. The night offered no answers, only the silent promise of another day to face. The kiss had been a catalyst, setting in motion a series of events that neither of us had anticipated. And as I lay down, the question of what came next loomed large, an unresolved melody in the symphony of our shared experience.

When Liam approached, his presence was like a thundercloud rolling in, dark and heavy. He offered a terse nod, his eyes avoiding mine as he walked past. I could feel the heat of his anger, though he said nothing. The weight of the kiss lay between us, an unspoken accusation that neither of us was ready to confront.

I tried to ignore the growing knot of anxiety in my stomach as I continued working. Every click of the camera felt like a reminder of our newfound estrangement, each shutter a snap that underscored the gap between us. The crew went about their tasks, oblivious or perhaps choosing to be, but the air was thick with the kind of tension that made it impossible to focus entirely on anything else.

At lunch, I sat with a group of crew members, their chatter a background hum as I picked at my food. I could see Liam at the far end of the table, his gaze fixed on his plate, his mood so unlike his usual self that it was almost jarring. We were no longer the team that had worked seamlessly together; instead, we were two people who had shared a moment that now seemed to divide us more than it ever had brought us together.

I stole glances at Liam, trying to gauge if there was any chance of reconciliation, but every time our eyes met, he looked away quickly, as if the brief contact might ignite something neither of us was ready to handle. I wanted to bridge the gap, to talk through what had happened, but the words seemed trapped behind a wall of pride and fear.

The afternoon dragged on, each minute stretching out in a painful reminder of the space that had opened up between us. I could sense that something had shifted in the way Liam interacted with everyone, not just with me. He was quieter, more withdrawn, his usual charisma dampened by an internal struggle that I could only guess at.

By the time the sun began to set, painting the sky with shades of orange and pink, I felt the exhaustion of a day spent in emotional limbo. The villa, which had once felt like a haven, now seemed to amplify the distance between us. I longed for the simplicity of the days before the kiss, when everything had been clear and uncomplicated. But that clarity was now clouded by a new reality that neither of us seemed prepared to face.

As I wrapped up for the day, Liam's figure appeared in the doorway, silhouetted against the fading light. He was dressed for the evening, his clothes more formal than usual, as if he were preparing for something important. He hesitated for a moment, his eyes meeting mine with a mix of uncertainty and resolve.

"I need to talk to you," he said, his voice carrying a weight that made my heart skip. There was something different in his tone, a softness that had been absent all day. I nodded, trying to keep my composure despite the pounding of my heart.

We walked outside, the cool night air a stark contrast to the suffocating tension of the day. We didn't speak as we made our way to a quiet spot by the edge of the villa, where the view of the stars offered a sense of calm and isolation. Liam leaned against a stone wall, his hands buried in his pockets, as if searching for the right words.

"I'm sorry about this morning," he began, his voice low and rough. "I didn't mean to make things so awkward."

I shook my head, trying to find the right words to express what I felt. "It's not just about this morning. It's... everything. We crossed a line, Liam, and I don't know what to do now."

Liam sighed, running a hand through his hair. "I know. I've been thinking about it all day. I didn't expect things to go this way. I didn't expect to..."

He trailed off, leaving the sentence unfinished. I could see the struggle in his eyes, the internal conflict that mirrored my own. It was as if we were both grappling with the consequences of our actions, trying to make sense of something that had suddenly become so complicated.

"I never meant for any of this to happen," he said finally. "I didn't want to mess things up between us. But I can't pretend like nothing happened. I care about you, Ava. More than I should."

The confession hung in the air, its weight heavier than I had anticipated. I looked away, trying to gather my thoughts. The honesty in his words was both a relief and a burden, a glimpse into the vulnerability he had been hiding behind his carefully constructed facade.

"I care about you too," I admitted, my voice barely more than a whisper. "But we need to figure out what this means. We need to understand what comes next."

Liam nodded, his expression a mix of relief and apprehension. "You're right. We need to talk about it. We need to be honest with each other, and with ourselves."

As we stood there, the night settling around us, it felt as though the space between us was slowly beginning to close. The conversation was far from over, but it was a start. And for the first time in what felt like an eternity, I felt a flicker of hope that we might find a way through the fallout and into something new—something that was, for better or worse, more real than anything we had shared before.

By evening, the villa's usual warmth felt cold and distant. The hum of cicadas outside was a constant reminder of how normal everything should be, juxtaposed against the dissonance I felt inside. I knew I had to address the elephant in the room, but every attempt to start a conversation with Liam seemed to falter before it even began.

As the sun dipped below the horizon, casting a golden haze over the ocean, I found myself wandering the grounds aimlessly. My footsteps were the only sound, a rhythmic echo that matched the rhythm of my restless thoughts. I needed clarity, an answer to the questions that had been swirling since that kiss, but the answers seemed to elude me as much as Liam's gaze did.

I found him on the edge of the terrace, his profile outlined against the darkening sky. He stood there like a statue, lost in his thoughts. My heart twisted at the sight of him, so close yet so far away. I hesitated for a moment, fighting the urge to turn back, but something pushed me forward.

"Liam," I said softly, my voice barely a whisper. He turned to face me, and in that instant, I saw a flash of vulnerability in his eyes that I hadn't noticed before. It was a stark contrast to the guarded persona he had maintained throughout our time together.

He looked at me with a mixture of surprise and apprehension. "Ava," he replied, his voice tinged with a weariness that mirrored my own. There was an awkward pause, the silence stretching out between us as we struggled to find the right words.

"I'm sorry," I began, the words tumbling out before I could second-guess them. "I didn't mean for things to become so complicated. I just—"

He cut me off with a raised hand. "No, it's not just you. I—" He sighed heavily, raking a hand through his hair. "I've been avoiding this conversation because I don't even know how to start. What happened... it's not something I can just brush aside. It's changed everything."

I swallowed hard, trying to process the weight of his words. "I know," I said, my voice trembling slightly. "I feel it too. But I don't want us to just ignore it. If we can't talk about it, then... what are we doing?"

Liam took a deep breath, his eyes locking onto mine with a newfound intensity. "I don't know what's going to happen next, Ava. But I do know that avoiding each other isn't going to solve anything." He stepped closer, the space between us shrinking with each step. "I want to be honest with you. That kiss... it meant something to me. More than I was prepared to admit."

My heart skipped a beat at his confession. "Me too," I admitted quietly. "But I'm scared. Scared of what it means for us, for this shoot, for everything we've worked for."

He reached out, his fingers brushing against mine in a gentle gesture that sent a shiver down my spine. "We can't ignore it," he said softly. "But we also can't let it destroy everything we've built. Maybe we need to figure out what this means for us, without letting it overshadow everything else."

I nodded, feeling a mixture of relief and trepidation. "I want that too," I said, my voice steadying as I spoke. "I want us to be able to move forward, whatever that means."

Liam's gaze softened, and he gave me a tentative smile. "Then let's take it one step at a time. We'll figure this out together."

In that moment, the weight of the kiss, the fallout, and the tension seemed to lift, if only slightly. We stood there, side by side, both of us uncertain but willing to face whatever came next. It wasn't a resolution, not yet, but it was a beginning—a chance to address the fallout and see where it might lead us.

Liam and I sat on the terrace, the sea sprawling before us like a vast canvas of blues and golds, the horizon melting into a soft blur where the sun had just set. The villa's lights were beginning to twinkle on, their glow warm but distant, mirroring the tumultuous feelings roiling inside me. The silence between us was heavy, charged with the gravity of the unsaid, as if the evening itself was holding its breath in anticipation.

His gaze was steady, searching, as he finally broke the silence. "We need to talk," he said, his voice low and firm, carrying an urgency that matched the clench in my stomach. I nodded, unable to find my voice, and we moved to a pair of wrought iron chairs that had been abandoned as the crew settled for the night.

We sat across from each other, our knees almost touching, the space between us both intimate and intimidating. I could see the way the evening light played across his features, highlighting the shadows of doubt and resolve. His eyes, usually so self-assured, now looked vulnerable, and for the first time, I saw the real Liam—the one who wrestled with the same insecurities and fears I did.

"I can't stop thinking about you," he said, his eyes locking onto mine with an intensity that made my heart race. The admission hung in the air, bold and unyielding, and I felt my own feelings reflected back at me. I swallowed hard, the lump in my throat a painful reminder of how much this moment mattered.

"I..." My voice faltered, betraying the swirl of emotions within me. "I feel the same way, but this is so complicated. We've crossed a line, and I don't want to ruin everything."

His gaze softened, but his expression remained conflicted. "I know it's complicated. I've been trying to ignore it, to pretend like it's not real, but it is. And I can't just shut it off." He leaned forward slightly, his hands gripping the edge of his chair. "I think about you all the time. The way you look at me, the way you laugh, the way you care about things. It's like you see me for who I really am, not just the image I've carefully crafted."

The vulnerability in his voice was a stark contrast to the strong façade he usually maintained. It shook me, and I could feel my own defenses crumbling. I had been so scared of this moment, of the confrontation that would force us to confront what had happened between us and what it meant for the future.

"I'm scared too," I admitted, my voice barely above a whisper. "I don't want to lose what we've built here. The project, the trust, everything. It's all so important."

He nodded, understanding the weight of my words. "I get it. This is more than just about us It's about the impact on everything around us. But I also can't ignore what's between us. It feels like there's something real here, something that's not just going to disappear because we try to pretend it never happened."

The honesty in his words was both a comfort and a torment. I wanted to reach out, to close the distance between us, but the fear of the consequences held me back. What if this was a fleeting moment, a spark that would fizzle out and leave us with nothing but regrets?

"I don't know what to do," I said, tears threatening to spill over. "I want to be with you, but I'm terrified of making things worse. What if this changes everything and we can't go back?"

Liam's expression was pained, and he reached out, his hand brushing against mine in a gesture of solace. "I don't have all the answers either. But I know that ignoring this, pretending it's not real, isn't going to help either. We need to face this, figure out what we want, and decide if we're willing to take the risk."

His touch was electric, sending shivers down my spine. The warmth of his hand on mine was a tangible reminder of how deeply connected we were, despite the fear and uncertainty. I wanted to believe that we could find a way through this, but the stakes felt so high, and the fear of losing everything loomed large.

The fading light of the evening wrapped around us like a cocoon, a temporary shield from the chaos of our emotions. As we sat there, our hands intertwined, I felt a glimmer of hope, mingled with the anxiety of what lay ahead. We were standing on the edge of something profound, and the path forward was uncertain. But in that moment, as we faced the reality of our feelings, I realized that whatever we decided, it would be a journey we had to take together.

His confession seemed to hang in the air, settling around us like the evening mist that was beginning to roll in off the sea. My heart pounded, each beat a reminder of the vulnerability we were both exposing. Liam's gaze was unwavering, his eyes reflecting a vulnerability I hadn't seen before. He was raw, stripped of the defenses he had so meticulously built.

"I know this isn't easy," Liam said, his voice low, almost as if speaking any louder might shatter the fragile moment we were sharing. "But I can't pretend like nothing happened. I can't go back to how things were before." He sighed, a sound of deep resignation mixed with hope. "It's like everything's changed, and I don't know how to go back to the way things were. Maybe I don't even want to."

I felt a pang of fear at his words. Everything had changed—there was no denying that. But the fear of losing what we had, of completely upending our lives, was almost too much to bear. I had come to cherish the routine, the predictability of our days, and the thought of disrupting it for something so uncertain made my chest tighten.

"You're right," I said softly, trying to steady my trembling hands. "We can't go back. But moving forward... what does that even look like? What happens now?" I felt tears pricking at the corners of my eyes, the reality of our situation pressing down on me. "I'm scared, Liam. Scared of making a mistake that could ruin everything."

Liam's expression softened even more, and he reached out, his hand gently touching mine. The contact was electric, sending a shiver up my arm. "I'm scared too," he admitted. "I don't want to lose what we have, but I also can't ignore how I feel about you. I don't want to pretend that this isn't real." His thumb brushed lightly against the back of my hand, a soothing gesture that made my heart ache with longing.

I looked down at our joined hands, the warmth of his touch grounding me amid the storm of my thoughts. "What if we're wrong? What if we're just setting ourselves up for more pain?" The question hung between us, heavy and uncertain. I wanted to believe in the possibility of something more, but doubt clung to me like a persistent shadow.

Liam sighed deeply, his gaze never leaving mine. "Maybe we are. But isn't it worth the risk? I've never felt this way about anyone before, Ava. It's like you've broken through something I didn't even know was there." He paused, searching for the right words. "I can't promise that everything will be perfect or that there won't be challenges, but I know that I don't want to walk away from this without at least trying."

I took a deep breath, my mind racing as I weighed his words. I had never been one to leap without looking, to embrace uncertainty with open arms. But Liam's honesty, his willingness to confront his fears and feelings, was both terrifying and deeply compelling.

"I want to try," I said finally, my voice steady despite the trembling in my heart. "I want to see where this can go. But we need to be honest with each other, about everything. About what we want, about what scares us, about what happens if things don't go as planned."

Liam nodded, his eyes filled with a mixture of relief and determination. "Absolutely. We'll face it together, whatever comes." He squeezed my hand gently, a promise of solidarity in the midst of the uncertainty.

The sea continued its gentle lullaby in the background, the waves softly crashing against the shore, a calming presence as we sat there, our hands still intertwined. The weight of the decision we had made hung heavily, but there was also a new kind of lightness in our shared resolve. It was a beginning, uncertain and fraught with potential pitfalls, but a beginning nonetheless.

As we sat together in the fading light, I felt the first tentative stirrings of hope amidst the fear. The path ahead was still shrouded in ambiguity, but for now, the most important step was taken. We had chosen to face it together, and that was a start—a fragile, hopeful start.

The silence that followed was heavy, like the thick, humid air before a storm. Liam's hand was still holding mine, and I could feel the warmth seeping into me, a stark contrast to the cold fear curling in my stomach. I wanted to pull away, to create distance between us, but his touch anchored me to the moment, to the truth of what we had done.

"I don't know if I can handle this," I whispered, my voice barely audible over the distant crashing waves. "I don't know if we're strong enough to face whatever this might turn into." The words were like a confession of my deepest fears, laid bare for him to see.

Liam's grip tightened slightly, and he leaned in, his breath warm against my cheek. "I don't have all the answers," he said quietly. "I just know that I can't ignore what's between us. I can't pretend it didn't happen. We both felt it, and we both need to figure out what it means."

His words were like a balm to my wounded heart, but they also left me feeling more exposed than ever. I closed my eyes, trying to steady my racing thoughts. "I don't want to lose what we have," I said, the vulnerability in my voice unmistakable. "But I'm terrified of what might happen if we let this... whatever this is, continue."

Liam's hand moved up to gently cup my face, his touch tender and reassuring. "We don't have to figure everything out right now," he said, his voice firm yet gentle. "We can take it one step at a time. All I'm asking for is a chance to see where this could go, to see if we can make it work."

I looked up into his eyes, searching for a glimpse of the certainty that seemed to elude me. All I saw was a deep, unwavering sincerity. "I'm scared, Liam. I'm scared of getting hurt, of making things worse than they already are."

He nodded, his expression one of understanding and empathy. "I'm scared too," he admitted. "But I'm more afraid of letting this chance slip away without at least trying. We owe it to ourselves to explore this, to see if what we have is worth fighting for."

The sea continued to stretch out before us, a vast expanse of uncertainty mirroring the chaos inside me. I took a deep breath, trying to calm the storm of emotions swirling within me. "Okay," I said finally, my voice trembling but resolute. "We'll take it one step at a time. We'll see where this leads, but we have to promise each other that we'll be honest, that we won't let this turn into something it shouldn't be."

Liam's face lit up with a small, hopeful smile. "I promise," he said. "We'll be honest with each other. We'll face whatever comes our way together."

As he spoke, I felt a small but significant shift within me. The fear was still there, but it was now tempered with a glimmer of hope. The walls that had seemed so impenetrable just moments before began to feel a little less daunting. Maybe, just maybe, there was a way through this chaos.

We sat there for a while longer, our hands still intertwined, the sea a witness to our unspoken vows. The sun dipped lower on the horizon, casting a golden hue over the water, as if trying to offer us some reassurance. I knew that whatever lay ahead, we were no longer facing it alone. And for the first time in days, I allowed myself to hope that maybe, just maybe, we could find a way to navigate through the uncertainty together.

The stars began to appear in the darkening sky, their light flickering like the fragile hopes we held. As we stood up and headed back inside, our steps were lighter, and the air between us felt less heavy. We were still treading unknown waters, but at least now, we were doing it side by side.

The days that followed were a strange blend of normalcy and tension. The crew continued their work with the same dedication, their laughter and chatter filling the villa, but for Liam and me, the days were marked by a quiet intensity. We navigated our interactions with careful precision, like two dancers attempting a complicated routine without stepping on each other's toes. We avoided private conversations, exchanged only polite smiles in public, and clung to the pretense of normalcy while the weight of our shared secret loomed over us.

Each day brought with it a new layer of complication. The subtle glances, the stolen touches, and the unspoken words that lingered between us were a constant reminder of what we were both trying to ignore. We had both become experts at masking our emotions, but it was exhausting. The exhilaration of our kiss had been replaced by a slow, creeping fear of what would come next. We were constantly on edge, trying to maintain the delicate balance between our personal feelings and our professional lives.

Then came the evening when everything changed. The sun was setting over the cliffs, casting a golden hue over the landscape, painting the sky with hues of orange and pink that seemed almost unreal. The beauty of the scene was a stark contrast to the tumultuous emotions brewing inside me. I found myself standing alone on the terrace, the cool breeze ruffling my hair, when Liam approached me. His presence was like a magnet, pulling me toward him with an irresistible force.

"Can we talk?" he asked, his voice low but firm. There was an urgency in his tone that made my heart skip a beat. I nodded, unable to find the words to express the jumble of thoughts racing through my mind. We walked to a secluded spot on the edge of the terrace, away from the prying eyes of the crew. The sound of the waves crashing against the rocks below was a soothing backdrop to the storm of emotions we were about to confront.

Liam turned to me, his eyes locked onto mine with a determination that left me breathless. "I've been thinking a lot," he began, his gaze unwavering. "About us. About what happened. I know it's risky, and I know it complicates everything, but..."

He stopped, searching for the right words. I could see the struggle in his eyes, the way he was trying to articulate what he was feeling without making everything worse. The air between us was charged, thick with unspoken words and raw emotion. I felt my heart pounding in my chest, each beat echoing the uncertainty of our situation.

"I don't care about the consequences," Liam said finally, his voice steady. "I want you, Ava. I want us to be together, to see where this could go, regardless of what might happen. I'm willing to take the risk if you are."

His words hung in the air, a declaration of intent that was both thrilling and terrifying. I looked into his eyes, and for the first time since that night, I saw a clarity that was both comforting and daunting. My own feelings were a tangled mess of desire and fear, but his confession was like a beacon, guiding me through the confusion.

"I want you too," I admitted, my voice barely above a whisper. "But I'm scared. Scared of what this could mean for us, for our careers. I don't want to ruin everything we've worked for."

Liam took a step closer, closing the distance between us. His hand reached out to gently cup my cheek, his touch sending a jolt of warmth through me. "I know," he said softly. "I'm scared too. But I've never felt this way before. I've never wanted something so badly, and I'm willing to risk it all for the chance to see if this can work."

The sincerity in his voice was undeniable, and it mirrored the tumultuous emotions swirling inside me. The fear was still there, a shadow lurking in the corners of my mind, but it was overshadowed by the powerful force of our connection. The risk was enormous, but the potential reward was something I couldn't ignore.

I took a deep breath, trying to steady myself. "If we do this," I said slowly, "we have to be careful. We have to be prepared for whatever comes next, and we have to be honest with each other."

Liam nodded, his expression one of unwavering commitment. "I promise," he said. "We'll face this together. Whatever happens, we'll deal with it as a team."

In that moment, I knew that we were both willing to take the plunge, to embrace the risk and see where it led. The uncertainty was still there, lurking just out of sight, but so was the promise of something extraordinary. With Liam's hand in mine and the setting sun casting its last, warm glow over us, I felt a sense of resolve settle over me. The choice was made, and with it, everything had changed.

Liam's words hung in the air between us, their weight both thrilling and terrifying. The sky above was a riot of colors, the sun dipping low and setting the horizon ablaze with shades of orange and purple. I stood there, feeling the heat of the day transform into a cool evening breeze, yet all I could focus on was the intensity of Liam's gaze and the way my heart was pounding against my ribcage.

I had been trying so hard to ignore the growing connection between us, to convince myself that the risks outweighed the rewards. But his confession had shattered that illusion, laid bare the raw truth I had been hiding from even myself. His determination was palpable, a stark contrast to the uncertainty I had been feeling. I could see it in his eyes, the way he looked at me as though I was the only thing that mattered in the world.

"You don't mean that," I whispered, though I desperately wanted to believe him. My voice trembled, betraying the conflict raging inside me. "You're saying this now, but what about tomorrow? What about everything we've worked for?"

Liam stepped closer, closing the gap between us until I could feel the warmth radiating from his body. His hands reached out, cupping my face gently. The touch was electrifying, sending shivers down my spine. "I've thought about tomorrow," he said, his thumb brushing lightly against my cheek. "And I don't care. I don't want to look back and wonder what if. I want us to take this risk, to see where it leads."

His words were like a balm to my troubled heart, soothing the doubts and fears that had been building up inside me. The risk was enormous, but the way he spoke, the sincerity in his voice, made me believe that maybe, just maybe, it was a risk worth taking. I could feel the walls I had carefully built around my heart beginning to crumble, each brick falling away with the realization that I wanted this—wanted him—as much as he wanted me.

"What if we lose everything?" I asked, my voice barely more than a whisper. "What if this changes everything and we're left with nothing?"

Liam's eyes softened, and he shook his head slowly. "Sometimes," he said, his voice low and reassuring, "you have to risk everything to gain something that truly matters. I'm willing to take that chance with you. I believe in us."

His words struck a chord deep within me, resonating with the part of me that had been longing for something real, something that went beyond the superficial layers of our daily lives. I could see the vulnerability in his eyes, the way he was laying his own heart on the line, and it was impossible to ignore the pull I felt toward him.

I took a deep breath, gathering the courage I had been hiding from. "I want this too," I admitted, my voice steadying as I looked up at him. "I want us, even though I'm scared. I don't want to regret not taking this chance."

A smile spread across Liam's face, a smile that held a mix of relief and triumph. "Then let's take it," he said, his voice filled with determination. "Let's see where this leads us. We'll face the consequences together."

With those words, the last of my reservations melted away, replaced by a fierce sense of resolve. I nodded, the decision feeling both liberating and terrifying. Liam's smile widened, and he leaned in, his lips brushing against mine in a kiss that was soft and tender, yet filled with a promise of everything that lay ahead.

The kiss was like a seal on our decision, an affirmation that we were willing to face whatever came our way together. It was a moment of clarity amidst the chaos, a fleeting yet profound connection that made everything else seem insignificant.

As we broke apart, the world around us seemed to come back into focus, but it was different now. The sun had fully set, casting a deep blue hue over the sky, and the stars were beginning to twinkle above us, as if they were witnesses to our vow.

Liam took my hand, his grip firm and reassuring. "We're in this together," he said softly, his voice filled with certainty. "No matter what happens, we'll face it side by side."

And in that moment, with the night embracing us and the future uncertain, I felt a surge of hope. We were stepping into the unknown, but for the first time, it felt like we were doing it with purpose. Whatever lay ahead, I knew we would face it together, and that thought brought a sense of peace I hadn't felt in a long time.

Sometimes, you have to leap before you look, and in that moment, standing on the edge of everything I had built and everything I could lose, I felt like I was on the brink of something transformative. Liam's words echoed in my mind, the promise of something real and raw, but the fear of the unknown clung to me like a second skin.

His fingers were still gently cupping my face, and I could see the vulnerability in his eyes, a reflection of my own. It was as if the universe had conspired to bring us to this exact point, to force us to confront our deepest fears and desires. I knew he was right; I didn't want to look back and wonder what if. I wanted to be brave, to take the leap with him, to embrace the risk even if it meant potentially losing everything we had worked so hard to achieve.

The sun's last rays were fading, casting long shadows across the terrace, and the cool evening air was filled with the scent of the sea and the promise of a new beginning. I took a deep breath, steadying myself against the whirlwind of emotions. "Okay," I said finally, my voice steady but filled with the weight of the decision. "Okay, let's take this risk. But we have to be honest with each other, and we need to be prepared for whatever comes next."

A smile broke across Liam's face, a mixture of relief and triumph. He leaned in, his forehead resting against mine, and I could feel the warmth of his breath mingling with mine. "I'm ready for that," he whispered. "I want us to be honest, to be open. And whatever happens, we'll face it together."

In that shared breath, in that tender moment, the world outside seemed to blur and fade away. It was just us—two souls daring to embrace the unknown, to reach out and grasp at something we both needed but had been too afraid to fully admit. I felt a thrill of exhilaration at the thought of what could be, the possibility of something greater than either of us had imagined.

We kissed then, softly at first, a tentative exploration of the emotions that had been simmering between us. The kiss deepened, growing more urgent as our shared passion took over. Every touch, every sigh, was an affirmation of our decision, a confirmation that we were willing to navigate whatever consequences lay ahead.

When we finally pulled away, our faces were flushed, our breaths mingling in the cool evening air. The world felt different, charged with a new energy, a new sense of possibility. We stood there, wrapped in each other's arms, knowing that we had crossed a line but feeling more alive than we had in a long time.

"I don't know what the future holds," I said softly, looking up into Liam's eyes, "but I do know that I want to face it with you."

Liam's smile was a beacon of hope and determination. "And I want the same thing," he replied, his voice firm yet tender. "We'll face whatever comes our way, together."

The decision was made, the line had been crossed, and the future, though uncertain, felt promising. For the first time in what seemed like forever, I felt a surge of hope and excitement. The path ahead would be challenging, filled with obstacles and risks, but it was a journey I was ready to take with Liam by my side. The possibilities were endless, and though the road might be difficult, the chance to build something real and meaningful was a risk worth taking.

# Chapter 6:

The days that followed our decision were a whirl of stolen moments and fleeting encounters. The thrill of secrecy clung to us like a second skin, heightening every touch and glance with a charged intensity. It was exhilarating, this hidden world we had created for ourselves, but it was also fraught with the kind of tension that made my heart race in a way that felt both thrilling and terrifying.

Liam and I learned to navigate this new dynamic with a careful choreography. We'd exchange glances across the room, smiles that were just shy of too obvious, our fingers brushing as we passed each other in hallways. It was like living in a bubble, where the rules of our old lives had shifted, and we had to adjust to the new norms of our secret affair. The rest of the crew went about their business, oblivious to the undercurrent that electrified the space between us. It was a strange mix of relief and anxiety to know that our secret was safe, but that didn't keep the constant worry from gnawing at me.

Every stolen kiss, every quiet conversation under the stars, felt like a beautiful rebellion against the constraints of our public lives. The garden at the villa became our sanctuary, a place where we could shed our public personas and simply be ourselves. The moonlight painted everything in shades of silver, and the scent of blooming flowers mingled with the soft whisper of our voices. It was in these moments that I felt closest to Liam, where the world outside seemed to disappear, leaving just the two of us in our bubble of intimacy.

Yet, as much as I reveled in these stolen moments, there was always a shadow of doubt lingering at the edges of my mind. Each time we parted ways, I felt a pang of fear, a gnawing anxiety about what would happen if our secret was exposed. The thought of losing everything we had built, of facing the fallout of our actions, was a constant, unsettling presence. The stakes felt impossibly high, and the idea of risking it all for something that might not even last made my chest tighten with apprehension.

Liam, despite his open vulnerability with me, seemed to be wrestling with his own fears. There were moments when I would catch him looking off into the distance, his brow furrowed, as if grappling with the weight of our decision. It was as though he, too, was acutely aware of the fine line we were walking. Yet, his resolve never wavered. He would always come back to me with a reassuring smile, a promise of unwavering support, and a touch that spoke of the deep connection we shared.

The small, quiet moments we found together became increasingly precious, each one a reminder of the depth of our bond. But with each precious moment came a new layer of complexity. We had to be vigilant, constantly aware of the thin line we were treading. It was a delicate balance—keeping our secret while trying to maintain a semblance of normalcy in our public interactions.

One evening, as we sat on a secluded bench in the garden, the moonlight casting a soft glow around us, Liam took my hand in his. His touch was warm, his grip reassuring, but his eyes held a depth of emotion that spoke of both joy and concern. "Do you ever think about what happens next?" he asked softly, his voice almost a whisper.

I looked at him, feeling the weight of his question pressing down on me. "All the time," I admitted, my voice trembling slightly. "It's hard not to. I'm scared of what might happen if we're found out. But I'm also scared of losing what we have now."

Liam's gaze softened, and he gently squeezed my hand. "I know. But I want you to know that no matter what happens, I'm here with you. We're in this together, and we'll figure it out as we go."

His words were a balm to my anxiety, a reassurance that, for the moment, we were navigating this tumultuous journey together. The future was uncertain, fraught with risks and potential heartache, but in that garden, under the gentle glow of the moon, it was enough to simply be with him.

As we leaned in for a kiss, the world outside seemed to recede once more, leaving just the two of us, caught in a moment of fleeting but profound connection. The thrill of our secret lingered, mingling with the uncertainty of what lay ahead. But for now, all that mattered was the warmth of his touch and the promise of tomorrow, no matter how uncertain it might be.

Liam, despite his open vulnerability with me, seemed to be wrestling with his own fears. There were moments when I would catch him looking off into the distance, his brow furrowed, as if grappling with thoughts too heavy to voice. The carefree laughter we shared during those stolen moments seemed to fade into pensive silence when we were apart. I knew he was feeling the weight of our secret just as acutely as I was, and it only added to the tension that crackled between us.

One night, as we sat in the garden, the stars above our heads a silent witness to our quiet desperation, I noticed Liam's gaze lingering on the horizon. His fingers traced lazy patterns on the grass, a habit of his when he was deep in thought. The soft rustle of the leaves was the only sound that broke the silence between us. I reached out, placing a tentative hand on his arm, and he turned to look at me, his eyes troubled.

"Ava," he said softly, his voice barely above a whisper, "do you ever wonder if this was a mistake?" The question hung in the air, heavy with the gravity of his doubt. I searched his face, the moonlight casting shadows that only made his vulnerability more palpable.

I wanted to reassure him, to tell him that it was all worth it, but my own fears made it difficult to offer him the comfort he was seeking. "I don't know," I admitted, my voice trembling with honesty. "Sometimes it feels right, but other times I can't shake the feeling that we're just setting ourselves up for heartbreak." I squeezed his arm, trying to convey my sincerity. "But right now, I can't imagine not having you in my life."

His eyes softened, and he reached up to cup my cheek, his touch gentle but firm. "I know," he said, his thumb brushing softly against my skin. "I feel the same way. I just wish I knew how to make this easier. How to make the fear go away."

We sat there in silence for a while longer, our hands intertwined, as if holding on to each other was the only thing that made sense in the swirling chaos of our lives. The darkness around us seemed to mirror the uncertainty that loomed over us, a reminder of the risk we had taken and the delicate balance we now had to maintain.

The following days brought a mixture of bittersweet moments and fleeting happiness. Our encounters remained as passionate and intense as ever, but the weight of our secrecy cast a long shadow. We had to be cautious with every touch, every glance, knowing that the slightest slip could unravel everything. The exhilaration of our hidden relationship was tempered by the constant fear of discovery, and it was a tightrope we walked with growing apprehension.

Our interactions with the crew became more strained, as if we were all caught in a delicate dance of pretense. I found myself slipping into a role that felt increasingly alien, smiling and chatting with my colleagues while my mind was always half a world away, with Liam. The contrast between our public facade and our private reality became stark, and it was becoming harder to maintain the balance.

Liam, too, seemed to struggle with the duality of our existence. At times, he would appear distant and distracted, the weight of our secret pressing down on him. His usual confidence overshadowed by an undercurrent of anxiety, and I knew he was wrestling with the same fears I was. The fear of what would happen if our relationship was exposed, and the fear of losing everything we had built.

One evening, as we sat together in the villa's dimly lit lounge, the soft glow of the lamp casting a warm light over our faces, Liam turned to me with a determined expression. "Ava," he said, his voice steady, "I know this is hard, but I need you to know something. No matter what happens, I want you to remember that this—" He gestured between us, his eyes intense and sincere. "This was worth it. You're worth it."

His words struck a chord deep within me, and I felt a rush of emotion that made my eyes well up. I leaned in and kissed him, our lips meeting in a tender, lingering embrace that spoke of everything we couldn't put into words. In that moment, the fear and uncertainty seemed to dissolve, leaving only the certainty of our feelings for each other.

As we pulled away, I looked into his eyes and whispered, "I feel the same way, Liam. No matter what happens, I know that this was something special. And for that, I'm grateful."

We sat there together, holding on to each other as if our lives depended on it, the weight of our decision settling into the spaces between us. The future was uncertain, but in that moment, with Liam's arms around me and the warmth of our connection enveloping us, I found a sense of peace amidst the chaos.

# Chapter 7:

We sat on the edge of his bed, the room dimly lit by a solitary lamp. The quiet of the villa seemed to amplify the storm brewing between us, the silence heavy with the weight of our unspoken fears. I tried to read his expression, but his eyes were distant, as if he were searching for answers in the shadows on the walls.

"I'm sorry for how I acted today," he began, his voice barely more than a whisper. "I know it wasn't fair to you or to anyone else."

I didn't know how to respond. The anger and hurt from earlier were still fresh, but seeing him so raw, so vulnerable, made it hard to hold onto those feelings. "Liam, it's not just about the outburst," I said carefully. "It's everything. The way you've been lately... it's like you're unraveling, and I don't know how to help."

He ran a hand through his hair, a gesture of frustration and helplessness. "I thought I could handle it all—my career, this secret between us, everything. But it's harder than I imagined. I feel like I'm constantly walking a tightrope, and one misstep could bring it all crashing down."

His words were like a knife twisting in my heart. I had always admired his strength and confidence, but now I saw a side of him that was scared and unsure. The realization that this wasn't just about our romance but about his entire world coming apart left me feeling more lost than ever.

"I didn't mean to put so much pressure on you," I said softly, my voice trembling. "I never wanted to be the cause of your stress."

He looked at me, his eyes dark and troubled. "It's not just you. It's everything—the expectations, the constant scrutiny. I've never had anything like this before. I've always been in control of my life, but now... I don't know. I'm afraid of losing everything I've worked for."

The pain in his voice was palpable, and it resonated deep within me. I reached out, placing a hand on his, hoping to offer some comfort. "We don't have to do this alone. We can find a way to manage it, to make it work."

He squeezed my hand, his gaze meeting mine with a mixture of gratitude and fear. "I want to believe that. I really do. But I need to figure out how to balance everything without losing myself or pushing you away."

I nodded, understanding his struggle more than he might have realized. "We'll figure it out together. I don't want this—us—to be a burden. I want it to be something that makes us stronger, not weaker."

He smiled faintly, a hint of the old Liam returning. "You're right. I just need to be honest about how I'm feeling and not let it build up until it explodes."

The night wore on as we talked, our conversation moving from the surface issues to deeper, more personal fears. It was a cathartic experience for both of us, and though the answers weren't immediately clear, the act of sharing our vulnerabilities brought a new level of understanding between us.

As we finally settled into a quiet embrace, I felt a flicker of hope amidst the uncertainty. We were still facing significant challenges, but acknowledging them together felt like a step towards healing. In that moment, it was clear that while our paradise might have been marred by trouble, it was a place we could work through, as long as we faced it together.

The cracks in our relationship were real, but they were also a reminder of our humanity. In our quest to navigate the complexities of our connection, we had found something far more precious than just fleeting passion. We had discovered the raw, unfiltered truth of who we were—both the strength and the fragility. And in this truth, there was a chance for something more profound, something worth fighting for.

As I lay beside him, the night air carrying the distant sounds of the villa, I realized that while trouble had indeed come to our paradise, it was in the resolve to face it together that we might find our way back to a place of understanding and deeper connection.

He squeezed my hand, a gesture that seemed to anchor him in the sea of uncertainty he was drowning in. I could feel the tension in his grip, a reflection of the struggle he was battling internally. I wanted to be his solace, to ease his burden, but I was also grappling with my own fears and doubts.

"I know it's been hard," I said, trying to offer some semblance of reassurance. "And I understand why you're feeling this way. But we have to be honest with each other. If we keep pretending that everything's fine when it's not, it's only going to make things worse."

Liam nodded, his expression a mixture of relief and despair. "I just didn't realize how much I'd be affected by this. I thought I could compartmentalize everything—work, us, the secrecy. But it's all blurring together, and it's eating me up."

I could see the truth in his words. The pressure of keeping our relationship hidden, combined with the high stakes of his career, was creating a perfect storm. The very secrecy that had once thrilled us was now the source of our anxiety. It was as if the walls of our private world were closing in on us, and we were trapped within.

"I'm scared too," I admitted, my voice breaking. "I'm scared of what will happen if we're discovered, of how this might affect everything we've worked for. But I'm even more afraid of losing you, of letting this become something that drives us apart."

His eyes softened, and I could see the conflict within him—the desire to protect our relationship while also wanting to keep his career intact. "I don't want to lose you either," he said quietly. "But I don't know how to fix this. I don't want to keep making mistakes, pushing you away."

"We need to talk to each other more," I suggested, searching for a way to bridge the gap between us. "Not just when things are falling apart, but when we're trying to figure things out. We need to find a balance, a way to be together without letting it destroy us."

Liam took a deep breath, and for a moment, he seemed to gather his resolve. "You're right. We've been so focused on keeping everything hidden that we've neglected to address the real issues. We need to find a way to be open about our feelings, to communicate without fear of judgment."

The weight of his words settled between us, and I felt a glimmer of hope. It wasn't a complete solution, but it was a start—a chance to rebuild the trust and understanding that had started to erode. We needed to navigate this treacherous path together, to face the challenges head-on and find a way to keep our relationship strong.

"I want to make this work," I said, my voice steady despite the lingering uncertainty. "I want us to find a way to be together without it tearing us apart. But we have to be honest about our struggles, and we have to be willing to face them together."

Liam nodded, his expression more resolute. "I want that too. I'm willing to do whatever it takes to make this work, to be open and honest, and to find a way through this."

As we sat there, the quiet of the villa's garden enveloping us, I felt a renewed sense of determination. The road ahead was still fraught with challenges, but for the first time in a while, I felt like we had a chance. We had faced a critical juncture, and instead of allowing it to drive us apart, we had chosen to confront it together.

In the dim light of the evening, with the scent of blooming flowers in the air, I felt a small spark of hope flicker within me. It wasn't a guarantee that everything would be perfect, but it was a promise that we would face the future together, whatever it might hold. And for now, that was enough.

The secrecy was like a constant weight, pressing down on every moment we shared. Each day, the façade we wore grew heavier, and the cracks in our carefully constructed world widened. The crew's curiosity was a relentless force, their probing questions and sideways glances eroding the thin veneer of normalcy we clung to. The way Liam and I would sometimes lock eyes, only to quickly look away, only fueled the whispers and speculation. I could almost hear the gears turning in their minds, piecing together the puzzle of our increasingly erratic behavior.

We were meticulous in our attempts to maintain a professional distance. We laughed a little too loudly when we spoke in groups, made sure our conversations were always open and casual. But the effort to appear indifferent was exhausting, and I could feel the strain in my shoulders, in the forced smiles that never quite reached my eyes. The moments when we were alone, however, were filled with an intensity that made it hard to breathe. The stolen kisses behind closed doors, the whispered confessions in the quietest corners of the villa—all of it was a reminder of what we had to lose.

One evening, after a particularly grueling day of shooting, we found ourselves alone in the darkened villa garden. The moonlight cast a silvery glow over the neatly trimmed hedges and the twinkling lights strung across the trees. It was a beautiful setting, but the beauty felt hollow amidst the turmoil we were experiencing.

Liam took my hand and led me to a secluded bench, his grip warm against my chilled fingers. I could see the tension etched into his face, the lines of worry that had deepened over the past few weeks. We sat together in silence for a moment, both of us grappling with the heaviness of the situation.

"I hate this," he finally said, breaking the silence. His voice was rough, edged with frustration. "I hate that we have to hide, that we have to pretend. It feels like we're constantly walking on a tightrope, and one misstep could send everything crashing down."

I nodded, my heart aching at his words. "I know. It's like we're living in a constant state of anxiety. Every glance, every touch, feels like it's under a microscope. I'm so afraid that if anyone finds out, it'll all fall apart."

His eyes searched mine, looking for some reassurance, some sign that everything would be okay. "Do you think we're making a mistake?" he asked, his voice barely above a whisper.

The question was one I had been avoiding, a fear I didn't want to confront. But sitting there with him, the vulnerability of the moment made it impossible to hide from the truth. "I don't know," I admitted, my voice trembling. "Sometimes, I wonder if we're sacrificing too much for the sake of this... whatever it is between us. I keep thinking about what we stand to lose, and it scares me."

Liam's face softened, and he reached out to brush a stray lock of hair from my forehead. The tenderness in his touch contrasted sharply with the turmoil inside me. "I don't want to lose you," he said earnestly. "But I also don't want to lose everything we've worked for. I don't know how to find a balance."

The silence that followed was heavy, filled with the weight of unspoken fears and regrets. I wanted to find the right words to reassure him, to ease the anxiety that seemed to be consuming us both. But in that moment, all I could offer was my presence, the silent comfort of being there beside him.

"We'll figure it out," I said finally, though my voice was tinged with uncertainty. "We have to. We just need to be honest with each other and face whatever comes together."

Liam nodded, his grip on my hand tightening. "You're right. We need to face this, no matter how hard it is. I want to be with you, but we have to find a way to make this work without losing everything else."

As the night deepened and the stars sparkled above us, I clung to the hope that we could navigate this treacherous path. The secrets and lies that bound us felt like chains, but perhaps, if we could find a way to be honest and confront the challenges head-on, we could find a way through the darkness. The uncertainty of our situation remained, but in that quiet moment, I resolved to face it with Liam, no matter what the future held.

The pressure of our concealed romance grew unbearable. Each day was a delicate balancing act, a tightrope walk between maintaining appearances and succumbing to the magnetic pull that seemed to draw us together more intensely with each secret encounter. The crew's curiosity was a persistent, nagging force, making me acutely aware of every shift in behavior and every awkward silence.

One afternoon, as we huddled together in the break room, trying to avoid drawing attention, a fellow crew member, Sarah, offered a friendly smile. "You two seem quieter than usual," she remarked, her eyes darting between Liam and me. I managed a forced laugh, while Liam shifted uncomfortably beside me. "Just a long day," I said, hoping my voice didn't betray the lie.

But the truth was that we were anything but okay. The secrecy was tearing at the seams of our relationship, unraveling the once joyful moments into tense exchanges and forced smiles. I could see it in Liam's eyes too—the way they flickered with frustration, a silent plea for relief from the charade. He tried to be upbeat, to maintain his charm and easygoing demeanor, but the strain was beginning to show, a constant reminder that we were living a lie.

One evening, after another day of careful pretense and strained interactions, I found myself lying awake in bed, my mind racing with worries. The villa's walls seemed to close in around me, the silence of the night amplifying every creak and whisper. I couldn't escape the fear gnawing at my insides—the fear that one wrong move would expose us, unravel everything we'd built, and leave us with nothing but regret.

Liam's text pinged softly on my phone, breaking the quiet. A simple "Can we talk?" was all it said, but it was enough to make my heart race. I quickly threw on a robe and tiptoed downstairs, my breath coming in quick, nervous bursts.

He was waiting for me in the garden, the soft glow of the moonlight casting shadows over his face. As I approached, I could see the lines of exhaustion etched deeply into his features, the stress weighing heavily on his shoulders. "Hey," I said, trying to sound casual, though my voice betrayed my anxiety.

"Hey," he replied, his voice carrying a note of weariness. He took my hand gently, pulling me close as we sat on the familiar bench where we had shared so many intimate moments. The quiet of the garden seemed to offer a brief reprieve from the chaos of our daily lives.

"I've been thinking," Liam began, his eyes meeting mine with a seriousness that sent a shiver down my spine. "We can't keep this up. The secrecy—it's getting to me. I feel like I'm living in a constant state of fear, and I hate it. I hate that we have to hide."

I nodded, my heart aching at his confession. "I know. I feel the same way. It's like we're trapped in this never-ending game of pretending, and it's wearing us down. But what if—what if we're caught? What if the truth comes out and everything we've worked for is destroyed?"

Liam's grip tightened on my hand, a look of resolve crossing his face. "I don't know what will happen if we're caught. But I do know that this—" he gestured between us, his eyes filled with a mixture of hope and fear—"this is too important to just throw away. We need to decide what we want, truly. And if that means risking everything, then maybe we need to."

His words were a balm to my frayed nerves, a promise of something real amidst the tangled mess of our hidden lives. I could see the determination in his eyes, a fierce conviction that made me believe in the possibility of a future together, despite the risks.

I squeezed his hand, a silent agreement passing between us. "You're right. We can't keep living in fear. We have to make a choice, and whatever happens, we face it together. I'm willing to take that risk if you are."

Liam's expression softened, a mixture of relief and affection in his eyes. "I am. I want us to be honest, to stop hiding. It won't be easy, but I'd rather face whatever comes with you than continue like this."

As we sat together under the stars, the weight of our decision settled between us. We knew that the path ahead was fraught with challenges, but for the first time in a long while, there was a glimmer of hope. We were no longer just hiding from the world; we were preparing to face it together, ready to confront whatever secrets and lies lay ahead.

Liam's eyes searched mine in the dim garden light, reflecting a vulnerability that was both heartbreaking and raw. He took a deep breath, the kind that seemed to come from the depths of his soul, and his voice was low, almost a whisper. "Ava, I can't keep doing this. The secrecy, the constant worry—it's eating me alive."

I felt a shiver run through me at his words, a cold realization settling in my chest. The weight of our concealed relationship had become too much for both of us. It wasn't just the constant need to hide our feelings; it was the growing chasm between us, filled with unsaid words and unacknowledged fears. The more we tried to keep our secret, the more it seemed to erode the trust and intimacy we once shared so effortlessly.

"Liam, I know," I said softly, reaching out to touch his hand. The warmth of his skin was a stark contrast to the icy tension that had built up between us. "It's hard. Every glance we exchange, every time we have to pretend, it feels like we're tearing apart the very thing we're trying to protect."

He nodded, his expression one of resignation. "I thought I could handle it. I thought we could handle it. But the pressure's getting to me. I'm afraid that if we don't do something soon, we're going to lose everything. Not just our careers, but us."

The words hung in the air between us, heavy and laden with the reality of our situation. I had been clinging to the hope that things would somehow get easier, that we could find a way to make it work. But now, seeing the anguish in Liam's eyes, I couldn't deny the truth any longer. We were at a breaking point.

I squeezed his hand, trying to offer him the comfort that I felt slipping through my fingers. "I'm scared too," I admitted, my voice trembling. "I don't want to lose us, but I don't know how much longer we can keep this up."

Liam's gaze softened, and he pulled me into a tight embrace. His arms were strong, but they held a gentleness that made me feel safe even in the midst of chaos. "We need to find a solution," he said quietly. "Maybe it's time we face the consequences, whatever they may be. At least then we won't be living in constant fear."

I clung to him, the comfort of his presence a bittersweet reminder of what we had and what we might lose. "Are you sure?" I asked, my voice barely a murmur against his chest. "Are you ready for whatever comes next?"

He pulled back slightly to look into my eyes, his own filled with determination and a flicker of hope. "I am. I'd rather face the consequences with you than continue living this lie. It's too much. It's tearing us apart."

His words resonated deeply within me. Despite the fear and uncertainty, a part of me felt a glimmer of relief. The burden of secrecy had been stifling, and while facing the truth was terrifying, it was also a chance for us to finally be honest with ourselves and with everyone around us. It was a risk, but it was one we were both willing to take.

We stood there for a long time, wrapped in the quiet of the garden, each lost in our thoughts. The moonlight bathed us in its soft glow, casting shadows that seemed to dance in tandem with our thoughts. The world outside felt distant, as if it had shrunk to the size of the garden where we stood.

As the night wore on, we made a pact—one that was as much about facing the reality of our situation as it was about finding a way forward. We would confront the truth, no matter how daunting, and deal with the consequences together. It was a commitment to each other, to our relationship, and to the future we hoped to build.

Finally, with a deep breath and a renewed sense of resolve, we pulled away from each other. The path ahead was uncertain, but we had decided to take the first step. The weight of our secret was still there, but it was now overshadowed by the strength of our decision to face it together.

As we made our way back inside, the first rays of dawn began to lighten the sky, bringing with them the promise of a new day. Whatever awaited us, we knew we would face it with honesty and courage. And for now, that was enough.

The moon hung low in the sky, casting a silver sheen over the villa's sprawling terrace. The night air was warm and gentle, carrying the faint aroma of salt from the sea below. Liam and I had found solace in one of the private balconies, a small, secluded haven away from prying eyes. The world outside was still and serene, but inside, the atmosphere crackled with an intensity that seemed almost tangible.

We were wrapped in each other's arms, the boundary between us melting away with every shared kiss. Liam's touch was both urgent and tender, a paradox that made my heart race and my head spin. It was as if every moment of closeness was both a gift and a threat. We knew the risks, but in the privacy of the balcony, the danger felt distant, almost insignificant compared to the magnetic pull between us.

Liam's lips were warm against mine, a sensation I was slowly becoming addicted to. I could feel the tension of the day ebbing away, replaced by a sweetness that was dangerously close to making me forget everything but him. He pulled me closer, his hands cradling my face, his touch a gentle promise of something more.

Just as his kiss deepened, a sudden, sharp noise sliced through the tranquility. The sound of footsteps, hesitant and echoing off the stone walls, made my heart leap into my throat. I pulled away, eyes wide, and Liam's expression mirrored my own panic. We froze, barely breathing, as the footsteps grew louder, each one a drumbeat of impending disaster.

I glanced towards the entrance of the balcony, my pulse pounding in my ears. Through the dim light, I could make out the shadowy figure of one of the assistants, her silhouette momentarily framed by the doorway. For a few excruciating seconds, time seemed to stand still. The assistant's eyes were wide, her mouth opening slightly in shock as she took in the scene before her.

Liam instinctively moved to shield me, but it was too late for that. We were caught, if only for a brief moment. I could see the realization dawning on her face, the understanding that she had stumbled upon something she was not supposed to see. My breath caught, a silent plea on my lips for her to turn away, to forget what she had seen.

Then, as quickly as she had appeared, the assistant turned and fled, her footsteps retreating with hurried urgency. The silence that followed was deafening, punctuated only by the distant crash of waves against the cliffs. Liam and I remained frozen, our breaths coming in shallow, uneven gasps.

When I finally dared to look at him, the expression in his eyes was a mixture of relief and dread. We were safe—for now—but the close call had left a lingering sense of unease. The weight of what had just happened pressed heavily on my shoulders, a stark reminder of the fragile nature of our secret.

Liam took a deep breath, trying to steady himself, his hands still trembling slightly as he reached out to touch my cheek. "That was too close," he said, his voice strained. There was a vulnerability in his gaze that made me ache for him. "We can't keep doing this."

I nodded, my own fear mirroring his. "I know," I whispered. "But what do we do now? How do we fix this?"

The silence that followed was thick with unspoken fears and unresolved questions. I could see the turmoil in Liam's eyes, the frustration and uncertainty that had become all too familiar. We were standing on the edge of something we couldn't control, and the consequences of our choices were becoming increasingly unavoidable.

Liam's hand slipped into mine, a gesture of reassurance even as the weight of our predicament pressed down on us. "We need to figure out what's next," he said quietly, his voice steady but laced with worry. "We can't keep living in this constant state of fear."

I squeezed his hand, trying to offer the comfort I desperately needed myself. "I agree," I said softly. "We need to decide if this is worth the risk or if we need to find a way to make it work differently."

The night stretched on, and the stars above seemed to offer no answers, only a silent witness to our struggle. As we stood together, the reality of our situation loomed large, an inescapable truth that was both terrifying and poignant. The world around us had become a stage for our secrets, and the next steps we took would determine not only the future of our relationship but also the course of our lives.

The silence that followed the assistant's abrupt departure was heavy, almost suffocating. Liam and I remained frozen, our hearts racing in tandem, the intimate moment we had shared now shattered into a thousand pieces. The sound of her footsteps fading away was a cruel reminder that we had been given a fleeting second chance, one that came with its own set of consequences.

I could still feel the warmth of Liam's touch lingering on my skin, a stark contrast to the icy dread that had seeped into my bones. His eyes met mine, dark with a mixture of relief and anxiety. He ran a hand through his tousled hair, trying to regain his composure. I could tell he was as shaken as I was, though he was doing his best to hide it. The façade of control he wore was crumbling under the weight of our situation.

"Are you okay?" he finally asked, his voice rough but laced with genuine concern. I nodded, though the tightness in my chest made it hard to breathe normally. The reality of our situation was hitting me harder than ever. This close call was more than just a moment of fear; it was a glaring sign that we were treading on dangerous ground.

"I'm fine," I managed to say, my voice barely above a whisper. I moved to lean against the railing, trying to steady my nerves. The distant crash of the waves below seemed to mock the calm that I was desperately trying to cling to. The tranquility of the night, once so comforting, now felt like a cruel illusion.

Liam joined me, standing close but keeping a respectful distance. His gaze was fixed on the horizon, as if searching for answers in the darkened sky. The flickering lights from the town below added a touch of warmth to the cool night air, but they did little to ease the tension between us.

"I didn't think we'd get caught," he said, his voice low and strained. "I thought we were careful enough." His words were a mix of frustration and fear, an acknowledgment of how precarious our situation had become. I could see the internal struggle in his eyes, the same one I felt every time we stole away to be alone.

"It's not just about being caught," I said, trying to sound more assured than I felt. "It's about the risk of what could happen if the truth comes out." My mind raced with the potential fallout—the questions from the crew, the damage to our careers, and the most painful thought of all: what if this jeopardized what we had between us?

Liam's hand found mine, his touch grounding me in the midst of the chaos. "I know," he said softly, his thumb brushing over the back of my hand. "I know it's risky. But I also know that I can't just pretend like this isn't happening." His words were sincere, but they were laced with the uncertainty of a man who was grappling with a storm he hadn't anticipated.

We stood there for a while, in silence, letting the cool breeze and the distant sound of the ocean calm our racing hearts. I was overwhelmed by the feeling that we were on the brink of something significant, yet precarious. Every stolen moment, every secret glance, had led us to this point where the stakes were higher than ever.

Eventually, Liam spoke again, his voice firmer this time. "We need to be more careful," he said. "This can't keep happening. I can't keep feeling like we're living on borrowed time." His gaze was steady, but there was an underlying fear that I understood all too well. The thrill of our secret rendezvous had turned into a burden, a weight that neither of us had anticipated.

I nodded, squeezing his hand in a gesture of mutual understanding. "We will be," I promised, though I knew the path forward was anything but clear. The reality of our situation was setting in, and with it came a daunting sense of urgency. We needed to decide how to navigate the tightrope we were walking—whether to continue in secrecy or face the truth head-on.

The night felt different now, the shadows around us seeming to press closer, as if conspiring to reveal our secrets. The distant lights of the town twinkled like distant stars, a reminder of the world we were trying so hard to keep at bay. Liam and I had a decision to make, and it was one that would define the course of everything we had been building.

As we stood together, the night sky above us, I could feel the weight of our choices pressing down on us. The thrill of the forbidden had been intoxicating, but now it felt like a double-edged sword. The secrecy that had once been exhilarating was now a looming threat, casting long shadows over our future.

Our time of hidden affection was drawing to a close, and the path ahead was fraught with uncertainty. But as I looked into Liam's eyes, I saw a determination that mirrored my own. We were in this together, and whatever happened next, we would face it as a unit, ready to confront the consequences of our choices.

"...it's about the fact that we can't keep living like this," I continued, my voice trembling slightly despite my effort to stay calm. The enormity of our situation was sinking in, the secret we had been trying so hard to protect now feeling like a fragile thread about to snap. The close call had shaken me more than I cared to admit, and the dread of what could come next was almost unbearable.

Liam's hand found mine, his grip firm and reassuring in the midst of the chaos of emotions. He turned to face me, his eyes searching mine for a flicker of understanding or perhaps a sign that everything would be alright. "I know," he said quietly, his voice a rough whisper against the backdrop of the night. "I know this can't go on forever. But I'm not ready to let go of us, not yet."

His words, while comforting, also added to the weight of our predicament. It was one thing to acknowledge the problem; it was another to figure out how to fix it. The longer we kept this secret, the more precarious our situation became. I felt a deep, gnawing fear that we might not only lose what we had but also face repercussions that we weren't prepared to handle.

"We need to be smarter about this," I said, trying to sound more resolute. "If we're going to keep this up, we have to be more careful, more strategic. We can't afford another slip-up." My mind raced with the possibilities of what could happen if our secret was exposed—scandals, broken relationships, irreparable damage to our careers. It felt as though every decision we made was a gamble, with our future hanging in the balance.

Liam nodded, his expression grim but determined. "I'll do whatever it takes," he said. "I don't want to lose you, Ava. I need you to know that." There was a sincerity in his eyes that both comforted and frightened me. We were walking a tightrope, each step fraught with the risk of falling.

As we stood there, the quiet night seemed to close in around us, a silent witness to our struggle. The distant lights of the town twinkled like stars, oblivious to the turmoil we were experiencing. It was in these moments of quiet that the reality of our situation became most stark.

"I don't want to lose you either," I admitted, my voice softening. "But we have to face the truth. This secrecy is tearing us apart." I could feel the tears welling up in my eyes, a mix of frustration and fear threatening to overflow. The pressure of maintaining our hidden relationship was becoming too much to bear, and the fear of what lay ahead was almost paralyzing.

Liam took a deep breath, his gaze steady as he looked at me. "We'll figure it out," he said, his voice holding a note of determination. "We have to. I know this is hard, but we've faced challenges before. We can face this one too."

His words were meant to be reassuring, but the fear of the unknown still loomed large. We were navigating a stormy sea, and every decision we made felt like it could tip the balance one way or the other. The close call with the assistant had been a stark reminder of how precarious our situation was.

The night air grew colder as we stood there, the once comforting sound of the waves now a reminder of the unpredictable nature of our situation. Liam's presence was a steady anchor in the storm, but even his strength couldn't completely dispel the anxiety gnawing at me.

As we finally turned to head back inside, the weight of our dilemma hung heavy between us. We needed a plan, a way to navigate the treacherous waters we were now in. Each step we took felt like it was leading us closer to a crossroads, and I couldn't shake the feeling that the choices we made in the coming days would determine the fate of everything we held dear.

In the dim light of the villa's hallway, our hands remained intertwined, a silent pledge of solidarity amidst the uncertainty. The road ahead was fraught with challenges, but as long as we faced it together, I held onto the hope that we might find a way through. The truth was that our secret could no longer be contained, and the consequences of our actions would soon catch up with us. But for now, we would hold on to each other, trying to make the most of the fleeting moments we had before everything changed.

The stress of keeping our relationship hidden finally took its toll. One evening, after a grueling day of shooting that had left us both on edge, the pressure reached its breaking point. The villa was eerily quiet, the soft hum of the air conditioning the only sound that accompanied our strained breathing. Liam and I had retreated to the secluded corner of the garden, seeking refuge from the noise and the relentless gaze of the crew. But instead of finding solace, we found ourselves caught in the first real argument of our relationship.

It started with something innocuous, as these things often do. Liam's increasing impatience during the shoots had been a source of growing tension between us. His temper had been short, his interactions with the crew strained. The small cracks that had begun to appear in our perfect facade now seemed to be widening, and I felt it in every nerve. We had managed to keep our private turmoil hidden from everyone else, but the strain was becoming too much for either of us to bear alone.

"It's not just about you, Liam!" I said, my voice sharp with frustration. "It's about the way you've been treating everyone lately. You're shutting down around the crew, and it's making things worse for both of us." My heart pounded in my chest, a mixture of anger and hurt simmering beneath the surface.

Liam's eyes flashed with defensiveness. "You think this is easy for me?" he shot back, his voice rising. "I'm risking everything for this—our relationship, my career. It's not just about what's happening here; it's about the whole damn world watching us!"

The words hung heavy in the air, the intensity of the moment making my chest tighten with each breath. His accusation stung more than I expected, cutting through my own frustrations and fears. For a moment, I wondered if we had made a colossal mistake. Had our desire to keep this relationship hidden, this secret love that felt so perfect, now become a source of deep-seated resentment and anger?

"I'm not saying it's easy for me either," I replied, struggling to keep my voice steady. "But I can't keep pretending everything's fine when it's clear that it's not. We're both on edge, and it's affecting everything around us."

Liam's gaze softened slightly, though the tension didn't entirely dissipate. "I don't want to fight with you, Ava," he said quietly, though the frustration was still evident in his tone. "I just... I don't know how to fix this. I thought we were on the same page, but it feels like we're drifting apart."

The silence between us grew heavy, the words we had exchanged reverberating through the quiet night. The air was thick with unspoken emotions, the weight of our unvoiced fears and doubts pressing down on us. I could see the strain etched into Liam's face, the vulnerability that he tried so hard to hide. And I knew that I wasn't any better, my own insecurities and worries bubbling to the surface in this heated confrontation.

"I don't want to lose you," I said softly, the confession coming out in a whisper. "But I need us to be honest with each other. We can't keep pretending that everything is perfect when it's clearly falling apart."

Liam looked at me, his eyes reflecting a mixture of regret and sadness. "I know," he said, his voice almost breaking. "I just wish there was an easier way to do this. I'm scared, Ava. Scared that we're going to mess this up and lose everything we've built."

The vulnerability in his voice cut through my anger, and I felt my own resolve start to waver. We stood there in the darkness, the garden around us seeming to close in, and for a moment, I felt utterly alone despite the closeness of our shared space. The reality of our situation—how precarious it was, how delicate—became glaringly apparent.

"I'm scared too," I admitted, my voice trembling slightly. "But I believe in us. I believe that if we can just be honest with each other, if we can find a way to face this together, we can get through it."

Liam's shoulders slumped slightly, and he took a deep breath, as though trying to steady himself. "I want to believe that too," he said quietly. "I just need to figure out how to make it work without losing everything we've fought for."

The silence that followed was different from before. It was a quiet filled with a tentative hope, a recognition of our shared fears and a mutual desire to find a way through the darkness. We stood there, our anger and hurt slowly giving way to a fragile understanding. The night seemed to hold its breath, and I could feel the weight of our struggle pressing down on us, but there was a flicker of something else as well—a glimmer of hope that maybe, just maybe, we could navigate this storm together.

The silence that followed our heated words felt like a tangible thing, wrapping around us, thick and suffocating. My heart was racing, my breath coming in uneven bursts as I tried to make sense of the anger and hurt that had exploded between us. Liam's eyes, usually so full of warmth, now held a hardness that I had never seen before. He ran a hand through his hair, the gesture raw with frustration.

"I didn't mean to snap at you like that," Liam said finally, his voice softer but still tinged with a hint of exhaustion. He looked at me with an expression that was both apologetic and vulnerable, the walls he had built up cracking slightly. "I just—" he paused, searching for the right words. "I don't know how to balance this. Everything feels so out of control."

I could see the weight of his words, the strain etched into his features. It mirrored my own sense of being overwhelmed, of trying to juggle the demands of a hidden relationship with the pressures of our work. The secrecy was supposed to be a thrilling escape, a passionate undercurrent to our days, but it had turned into a nearly unbearable burden.

"I know," I said quietly, trying to keep the tremor out of my voice. "I feel it too. I thought we could handle this, but it's becoming too much. The pretending, the constant watching our backs—it's exhausting."

Liam took a deep breath, his shoulders sagging slightly as if the weight of the world had settled on them. He reached out and gently touched my arm, his touch light but full of meaning. "Maybe we're not as prepared as we thought we were. I thought I could handle the pressure, but it's like every moment I'm afraid of being found out, afraid of what it could mean for us."

I looked at him, my heart aching at the sight of his vulnerability. The man who usually seemed so confident, so in control, was now revealing a side of himself that was raw and uncertain. It was a stark contrast to the fiery anger from moments before. "Liam, I don't want this to break us. I don't want us to become something that we can't salvage."

He nodded, his gaze never leaving mine. "Neither do I. I think we both need to step back and figure out how to make this work without it tearing us apart. Maybe we need to be more honest with each other about what we're feeling, even if it's uncomfortable."

I nodded in agreement, feeling a bit of relief at his words. It was clear that we needed to communicate more openly, to address our fears and frustrations instead of letting them fester and explode. "I think we need to be honest about what's happening and how it's affecting us," I said softly. "Maybe if we stop hiding, even just a little, it won't feel so suffocating."

Liam's eyes softened, a hint of the old warmth returning as he looked at me. "You're right. I'm sorry for snapping earlier. I'm just scared. Scared of losing everything we have, and scared of the unknown."

I stepped closer to him, closing the distance that had felt so vast moments before. "I'm scared too," I admitted. "But we can't let fear control us. We need to face this together."

He pulled me into an embrace, his arms wrapping around me with a tenderness that felt like a balm to my wounded heart. I could feel his heartbeat against my chest, a steady rhythm that reassured me that despite everything, we were still connected. "Let's take it one step at a time," he murmured into my hair. "We'll figure this out. Together."

The simple act of holding each other, of sharing our fears and vulnerabilities, seemed to dissolve some of the tension that had built up between us. The weight of our argument still lingered, but it felt more manageable now that we had taken a step toward understanding each other better. The path ahead was uncertain, and the pressures of our hidden relationship remained, but in that moment, there was a flicker of hope.

As we stood there in the quiet of the garden, the night wrapping around us like a comforting cloak, I knew that our journey was far from over. The road would be rocky, the challenges daunting, but facing them together was the only way forward.

The silence lingered, stretching out like an uninvited guest that refused to leave. Liam's frustration had left an echo that seemed to fill the space around us, making it hard to breathe, to think. I could see the tension in the way he held himself, the way his jaw was clenched as if he was trying to physically hold back the emotions he couldn't quite control.

I took a step back, needing to create some distance between us, trying to regain my composure. My mind raced, trying to find a way to bridge the gap that had opened up between us. It wasn't just the fight that had shaken me—it was the realization that we were navigating uncharted waters, our relationship tested in ways we hadn't anticipated.

"I didn't mean to make this harder for you," I said, my voice barely above a whisper. "I just needed to be honest about how I'm feeling. I'm scared, too. I'm scared that all of this—us—will be for nothing if we can't find a way through it."

Liam's eyes softened, the hardness giving way to something more tender, more vulnerable. He moved closer, closing the gap I had created, his expression a mix of regret and concern. "I'm sorry. I didn't mean to lash out. It's just that... every day feels like a tightrope walk. I don't know how to handle the stress of hiding us and still trying to do my job. And seeing you upset makes it worse."

I nodded, feeling the sting of tears threatening to spill. "It's not just you. I'm struggling too. I thought we were strong enough to handle this, but it feels like the secrecy is turning us into something we never intended. I miss the way things used to be, when it was just us being ourselves."

Liam reached out and gently cupped my face in his hands, his touch a balm to the hurt we were both feeling. "I miss that too. I miss not having to worry about every little thing, about every glance or touch being scrutinized. I want us to be able to be ourselves, without fear."

The sincerity in his voice broke something open inside me. I reached up and placed my hands over his, holding them close. "Maybe we need to figure out a different way to handle this. Maybe hiding isn't the solution. Maybe we need to find a way to be honest, even if it means facing the consequences."

Liam's eyes searched mine, looking for something—reassurance, perhaps. "Do you think we're ready for that? To face what comes next?"

I took a deep breath, feeling a mix of apprehension and determination. "I don't know if we're ready, but I know we can't keep living in this constant state of fear and uncertainty. It's tearing us apart."

He nodded, his grip on my face tightening slightly as if he was drawing strength from my resolve. "You're right. Maybe it's time to stop running from the truth and start facing it, whatever that means for us."

We stood there in the dim light of the room, the tension between us still palpable but now tempered by a newfound sense of understanding. The argument had opened up a space for us to confront the reality of our situation, to acknowledge the strain and the fear, and to make a choice about how we wanted to move forward.

"I don't want to lose you," Liam said softly, his voice breaking the silence that had settled over us. "And I don't want us to be defined by the secrets we keep."

I squeezed his hands, feeling a flicker of hope despite the uncertainty that lay ahead. "Neither do I. We need to be honest with each other and with ourselves. Whatever happens, we face it together."

He nodded, his eyes filled with a mixture of hope and resolve. "Together."

We stood there, holding on to each other, the weight of the argument still lingering but now overshadowed by a commitment to face whatever came next. The path forward was uncertain, and the challenges of our hidden relationship remained daunting, but in that moment, we found a fragile but vital understanding. We were ready to confront the reality of our situation, to move forward with honesty and courage, whatever the outcome might be.

# Chapter 8:

I wanted to respond, to bridge the gap that had formed between us, but the words stuck in my throat. The room felt too small, too charged with the weight of everything we hadn't said. Liam sat there, his hands gripping the edge of the bed, his gaze fixed on the floor as if searching for answers in the carpet fibers.

"I don't want to lose you either," I finally managed, my voice barely a whisper. The honesty in my own admission surprised me. It was true—this wasn't just a fleeting attraction. What Liam and I had was deeper, more complex, and it scared me to think of it unraveling.

Liam looked up, his eyes meeting mine with a fierce intensity. "I've never been in a situation like this before," he said, the confession almost a plea. "I thought I could handle it, that I could keep everything together. But it's like every step we take forward, we're taking two steps back. I'm so afraid that if this continues, it's going to end up destroying everything we've built."

The rawness in his voice made my heart ache. I reached out, placing my hand over his. The touch was hesitant but reassuring, a silent acknowledgment of the storm we were weathering together. "We're both struggling," I said softly. "But that doesn't mean we should give up. We've come too far to let this tear us apart."

Liam's fingers tightened around mine. "I know," he said, his voice breaking. "But it feels like the more we try to keep this secret, the more it consumes us. I don't want to keep fighting against something we both feel so strongly. It's exhausting."

"I feel the same way," I admitted, my heart pounding with the force of my words. "But maybe we can find a way to navigate this. Maybe we can figure out how to make it work without losing ourselves in the process."

Liam's gaze softened, and he pulled me closer, wrapping his arms around me. I leaned into him, savoring the comfort of his embrace.

For a moment, the world outside ceased to exist. It was just us, tangled in our own emotions, trying to find a way forward.

"I want to believe that we can make this work," he said, his voice muffled against my hair. "I just don't know how."

I closed my eyes, taking a deep breath. "We don't have all the answers right now," I said. "But we have each other, and that's something worth fighting for. We just need to be honest with each other and with ourselves. Maybe that's where we start."

Liam pulled back slightly, his eyes searching mine. "What if we come clean about us?" he asked tentatively. "What if we stop hiding and let everyone see us for who we really are?"

The suggestion hung in the air, heavy with the potential for change. I felt a mix of fear and hope. The idea of exposing our relationship was daunting, but the prospect of living in constant secrecy was wearing us down.

"I don't know what will happen if we do that," I said slowly. "But I do know that I can't keep living like this. I need to be true to myself, and to you."

Liam nodded, his expression a blend of determination and uncertainty. "Okay," he said quietly. "Let's figure this out together. We'll face whatever comes our way, but we need to be honest about who we are and what we want."

The resolution between us felt like a small, fragile light in the darkness. It wasn't a guarantee of smooth sailing, but it was a start. We were both committed to facing our challenges head-on, and that was something.

As we sat there, wrapped in each other's arms, the night stretched out before us, filled with the unknown. But for the first time in a long while, I felt a flicker of hope. We had a chance to redefine our path, to rebuild what had been strained by secrecy and doubt.

And as I looked into Liam's eyes, I saw the reflection of my own hopes and fears. Together, we were embarking on a journey that promised to be difficult but also profoundly meaningful. We were on the edge of something new, and though the future was uncertain, we were ready to face it—together.

Liam's confession hung between us, heavy and unresolved. I could see the vulnerability in his eyes, a stark contrast to the confident persona he usually wore like armor. His shoulders sagged, the weight of his admission visibly exhausting him. I wanted to respond, to find the right words to ease his fears, but my mind felt clouded by the same uncertainties he had just laid bare.

"I don't want to lose you either," I said again, my voice a fragile thread connecting us. The truth of my words felt like a balm, yet the fear of what lay ahead gnawed at me. I looked up at him, trying to read his expression, searching for some hint of the way forward. His gaze met mine, and in that shared silence, I realized that we were both standing on the precipice of something monumental.

Liam shifted, his grip on my hand loosening just enough to allow me to see the raw emotion etched on his face. "It's like we're caught in this constant struggle between what we want and what's practical," he said, his voice a soft murmur against the backdrop of our strained silence. "I don't want to be just a secret. I want to be something real, something we don't have to hide."

His words cut through the haze of my own anxieties. I nodded, feeling a tear slip down my cheek. "I feel the same way. But how do we make it work? How do we keep this from consuming us when everything around us is against it?"

Liam took a deep breath, his eyes searching mine with a mix of hope and resignation. "Maybe we need to stop fighting against the world and start fighting for us," he suggested. "Maybe we need to figure out how to balance everything—our work, our lives, and this... us."

His suggestion sparked a flicker of hope within me. "You're right," I agreed, my voice steadier now. "We can't let this consume us.

We need to find a way to make it work without losing ourselves in the process."

We stood there, wrapped in each other's arms, our hearts beating in sync as we faced the daunting task ahead. The road wouldn't be easy, and there would be challenges we couldn't yet foresee, but for the first time in a long while, I felt a sense of determination.

Liam's arms tightened around me, his warmth a comforting presence. "We'll figure it out," he said softly. "Together. We just need to keep communicating, keep being honest with each other. And maybe, just maybe, we can find a way to make this work without losing everything we've built."

His words were a promise, a commitment to navigate the stormy waters of our relationship with honesty and courage. I clung to that promise, feeling a renewed sense of resolve. We might not have all the answers, and the future was uncertain, but for now, we had each other.

As we stood there, the silence between us was no longer oppressive but filled with the weight of shared understanding and unspoken resolve. Liam and I were no longer just two people caught in a web of secrets and lies. We were partners, facing the challenges ahead with a commitment to each other that transcended the difficulties we faced.

In that moment, with Liam's arms around me and his heart beating close to mine, I felt a profound sense of clarity. The road ahead would be filled with obstacles, but I knew that as long as we faced them together, we could find our way through.

# Chapter 9:

As we navigated the intricate dance of our growing intimacy, every shared laugh and whispered confession seemed to deepen our bond. Yet, the more I fell for Liam, the more the gnawing fear of our eventual separation haunted me. Our connection felt so intense, so significant, that the thought of losing it once the shoot ended was almost unbearable.

Liam and I would often find ourselves wandering through the winding streets of the picturesque Italian town, our hands brushing against each other in a gesture both casual and intimate. The soft murmur of conversation between us, punctuated by the occasional comfortable silence, felt like an escape from the pressures and expectations that surrounded us. It was during these walks that the weight of our secret seemed to lift, if only for a little while. We were free to be ourselves, to share unguarded moments away from the prying eyes of the crew and the ever-present threat of discovery.

One evening, as we strolled along a cobblestone path lit by the warm glow of street lamps, Liam stopped suddenly and took my hand in his. His touch was both tender and firm, as if he were trying to anchor himself in the midst of his own fears. "Have you ever thought about what happens after this?" he asked, his voice low and thoughtful.

I looked up at him, searching his eyes for some hint of the answer he was seeking. "All the time," I admitted. "I keep wondering if what we have will survive once we leave Italy. It feels so real here, so right, but what if it doesn't translate when we go back to our normal lives?"

Liam's gaze softened, and he squeezed my hand reassuringly. "I've been thinking the same thing," he confessed. "I don't know how to imagine life without you now. Everything feels different, better, when I'm with you. But the reality of our situation keeps hitting me—what if this is just a beautiful dream that ends when we wake up?"

The vulnerability in his voice mirrored my own fears, and it was both comforting and disheartening to know that he shared my anxieties. We were standing on the edge of something profound, something that felt like it could change both our lives, but the uncertainty of what lay beyond this chapter was daunting.

Despite our fears, there were moments when the intensity of our connection felt undeniable. The way Liam looked at me, as if he could see right through to the core of who I was, made me feel understood in a way I had never felt before. His touch, whether it was a simple brush of his fingers against mine or a lingering kiss, conveyed a depth of emotion that words couldn't fully capture. It was as if every interaction was a testament to how much we meant to each other, a silent affirmation of the bond we were forging.

Still, the looming shadow of reality remained. As we approached the end of the shoot, I could see the inevitable approaching—a return to our separate lives, the pressure of maintaining the façade of normalcy, and the daunting possibility that our relationship might not withstand the transition. Each day seemed to carry a weight of finality, a reminder that our time together was finite and that the clock was ticking.

I tried to push these thoughts aside, to focus on the present and cherish the moments we had left. Yet, the fear that this beautiful, intense connection might dissolve with the fading sunlight of our Italian adventure was a constant presence. I began to question whether the foundation we were building was strong enough to survive the realities of our lives back home.

In the end, our moments together became even more precious. Each shared experience, each laugh, each tender touch was a testament to what we had created. But with each passing day, the question lingered—what if this was all we had, a fleeting, magical moment that would eventually become a cherished memory rather than a lasting reality?

As Liam and I faced the twilight of our time together, I found solace in the depth of our connection, even as I grappled with the uncertainty of what lay ahead. The fear of losing him was palpable, but the strength of what we had built together gave me hope, even amidst the looming doubt.

Even as our connection grew, the shadow of our impending separation loomed over us, darkening the edges of our days together. The villa, with its stunning vistas and romantic nooks, became a cocoon where our fears were both comforted and heightened. Each day, we wove deeper into each other's lives, yet the knowledge that this would all end kept us both on edge, like actors caught in a rehearsal for a play with no final act written.

One particularly serene evening, after another long day of shooting, we found ourselves on the villa's rooftop terrace. The sun had dipped below the horizon, casting a twilight hue over the landscape. We had settled into the cushions of the lounge area, the soft fabric under our bodies contrasting with the crisp night air. Liam lay beside me, his hand tracing idle patterns on my arm, while I stared up at the first stars appearing in the sky. The silence between us was filled with a comforting intimacy, but also an unspoken tension.

"I can't help but wonder," Liam began, his voice breaking the silence with a hesitant edge, "if this is just a fleeting moment. You know, like a beautiful dream that we're both too afraid to wake from."

His words struck a chord deep within me, and I turned to face him, my heart aching with the weight of our reality. "Sometimes it feels that way," I admitted softly. "Like this place, this time with you—it's perfect, but it's also so fragile. I keep thinking that once we go back to our lives, everything will change. I don't want to wake up and find that this was all just an illusion."

Liam's gaze was unwavering, and he seemed to be searching for something in my eyes—something that would reassure him, just as I needed reassurance from him. "What if we could make it real?" he asked, his tone more determined than I had heard before. "What if we could take this—what we have—and find a way to keep it going, even after we leave?"

The question hung between us, fragile and profound. It was as if Liam was offering a lifeline, a way out of our collective fear of losing what we had found together. I wanted to believe it was possible, but the reality of our separate lives, our responsibilities, and the chaos of our careers seemed to stretch out before us, an unbreachable divide.

"I want to believe that," I said, my voice trembling with the weight of my hopes and fears. "I want to believe that we can take this with us, but it's so hard to imagine. We're both so entrenched in our own worlds, and they don't exactly make room for... us."

Liam sat up, his eyes locked onto mine with a fiery determination. "Then we need to figure out how to make room," he said. "We need to find a way to bring this—what we have—into our real lives. It's not going to be easy, but if we don't try, we'll never know if it's possible."

The intensity of his words struck me deeply, and for a moment, I felt a surge of hope mingled with fear. The idea of facing our separate worlds with this new connection was both exhilarating and daunting. Yet, the way Liam spoke, with such conviction and longing, made me believe that maybe, just maybe, we could find a way to make our dreams a reality.

We spent the rest of the evening talking, planning, and dreaming aloud about the possibilities. The stars above us seemed to listen, their twinkling lights a silent witness to our hopes and fears. As the night wore on, our conversation turned to lighter subjects, but the promise of what might come lingered between us, a glimmer of something real and tangible in the midst of our uncertainty.

By the time we finally parted ways to head to our separate rooms, there was a new resolve in the air. The fear of the unknown was still present, but it was tempered by a shared determination to see what we could build together. The night was quiet as I lay in bed, staring at the ceiling, but there was a flicker of hope in my heart—a belief that our story didn't have to end with the setting of the Italian sun.

The night air in the villa had turned cooler, the gentle breeze carrying the scent of the nearby sea. Liam and I had retreated to our favorite spot on the terrace, where the stars were more vivid and the world seemed to fall away. We had been talking for hours, our conversation slipping into deeper and more vulnerable territories with each passing minute. There was an intimacy to the night that made it feel like we were the only two people in existence, suspended in a moment that was both painfully beautiful and terrifying.

It was during one of these quiet moments, with the moonlight casting a silvery glow over Liam's face, that he finally broke the silence. His voice was barely audible, as if he was afraid that speaking too loudly might shatter the delicate balance of the evening. "I don't know if I can do this," he said, the words hanging heavy between us.

I turned to him, my heart racing. "What do you mean?" I asked, my voice trembling slightly as I reached out to grasp his hand. His fingers were cold, and I could feel the tension in them as he tightened his grip around mine.

He looked away, his gaze fixed on the horizon where the night sky met the dark, restless sea. "I've spent my whole life building this career," he continued, his words almost lost in the wind. "I can't risk losing it for something that might not last. I don't know if I can let go of everything I've worked for just for... us."

The depth of his confession cut through me like a knife. I had always known that Liam's career was his world, but hearing him voice his fears so openly was a shock. The realization of how precarious our situation was—the balancing act between his career and our relationship—made my chest tighten with an unfamiliar ache.

I had been so caught up in the whirlwind of our feelings that I had pushed my own fears to the back of my mind. But now, faced with the raw vulnerability of his confession, my own fears surged to the surface. I was scared, too. Scared of losing him, scared of what would happen if we didn't try, and terrified of the unknown future that loomed ahead.

Taking a deep breath, I turned fully to face him, searching for the right words. "Liam," I said softly, "I understand how much your career means to you. I know you've worked so hard to get where you are. But we're both standing on the edge of something incredible here, and I don't want us to let fear dictate our choices."

He met my gaze, his eyes filled with a mixture of hope and despair. "But what if this—what if we can't make it work? What if everything we have here is just a fleeting moment that can't survive outside of this bubble we're living in?"

I squeezed his hand tighter, willing him to see that there was more to us than just the fear of failure. "We can't know for sure what the future holds," I said, my voice steady despite the whirlwind of emotions inside me. "But what we do know is that right now, in this moment, we have something real. Something worth fighting for. You don't have to choose between your career and me. We can figure this out together."

His eyes searched mine, and for a moment, I saw the vulnerability and the longing that mirrored my own fears. The silence that followed was filled with the weight of his unspoken fears and my determination to make him see that we could overcome them together.

Finally, Liam spoke again, his voice softer but resolute. "I don't want to lose this, lose us. I just need to know that there's a way for us to have both—a future where we don't have to choose between what we've built and what we're building together."

I nodded, feeling a surge of hope mixed with the lingering uncertainty. "We'll find a way," I promised, my heart aching with the intensity of my feelings. "We have to believe that we can. And no matter what happens, we'll face it together."

As the night wore on, we remained on the terrace, holding each other close. The stars above seemed to shimmer with a newfound clarity, and for the first time in days, I felt a glimmer of hope. Despite the fear and the uncertainty, there was something undeniably precious about what we had. And even though the future was uncertain, the strength of our connection gave me the courage to believe that we could face whatever lay ahead, together.

The silence that followed his confession was heavy, almost unbearable. The stars seemed to dim as if they were retreating from the gravity of our conversation. I felt the weight of his words settle around us, pressing down like a tangible force. His fear was palpable, and for a moment, it was as if time itself had stopped, holding its breath in anticipation of what would come next.

Liam's gaze remained fixed on the horizon, his shoulders slumped in a way that made him appear smaller, more vulnerable. It was a side of him I hadn't seen before, the mask of confidence and control slipping away to reveal a man who was deeply afraid of losing everything he had worked so hard to achieve. It was both heartbreaking and illuminating.

I took a deep breath, forcing myself to stay calm despite the turmoil inside me. I reached out and placed my hand gently on his cheek, turning his face toward mine. His eyes, usually so steady and assured, were now clouded with uncertainty and fear. "You don't have to choose, Liam," I said softly, my voice steady despite the storm raging within me. "We can figure this out together."

His eyes searched mine, looking for something—hope, reassurance, maybe even a hint of the strength he was struggling to find in himself. I could see the conflict warring within him, the struggle between his career and the genuine connection we had forged. "But what if it's not enough?" he asked, his voice cracking. "What if I lose everything and still end up with nothing?"

The pain in his voice mirrored the fear in my heart. I had always known that our situation was precarious, but hearing him voice these fears so openly made the reality of it all the more stark. I wanted to reassure him, to offer him comfort and strength, but I also knew that the path forward was fraught with uncertainty.

I took his hands in mine, squeezing them gently. "I don't have all the answers," I admitted, my voice trembling with the weight of our shared fears. "But I do know that we have something real here. Something worth fighting for. And maybe we don't know how it will all work out, but that doesn't mean we shouldn't try."

Liam's expression softened slightly, though the fear didn't entirely leave his eyes. He seemed to be grappling with the idea of letting go of his carefully constructed plans and allowing himself to embrace the uncertainty of our future. "It's just... it's so hard," he said, his voice barely above a whisper. "I've always been in control, and now it feels like everything is slipping away."

I nodded, understanding more than I had before. His life had been meticulously planned, each step calculated and controlled. The spontaneity of our relationship, the unknowns that came with it, were in stark contrast to the ordered existence he had built for himself. It was no wonder he was struggling. "I know it's hard," I said softly. "But sometimes, the most beautiful things come from taking risks. From letting go and allowing ourselves to be vulnerable."

His gaze fell to our joined hands, his fingers curling around mine as if seeking solace in their touch. The moment stretched, and I could almost see him weighing the possibilities, the what-ifs of our situation. It was clear that the fear was still there, but I hoped that my words had offered a glimmer of hope, a hint of possibility.

"I want to believe that," he said finally, his voice filled with a mixture of hope and skepticism. "I really do."

I leaned closer, resting my forehead against his. "Then let's take it one step at a time," I said, my voice firm yet gentle. "We don't have to have all the answers right now. We just have to be willing to try, to fight for what we have. And whatever happens, we face it together."

For a long moment, we remained like that, wrapped in each other's presence, finding comfort in the shared silence. The night was still around us, the world holding its breath as we took a tentative step toward confronting our fears together. The road ahead was uncertain, but in that quiet moment, with our hearts laid bare and our fears acknowledged, I felt a sense of resolve—a promise to face whatever came next with courage and togetherness.

As the night wore on and the stars began to fade, we sat there in silence, but the unspoken understanding between us was a new kind of strength. It wasn't about having all the answers, but about being willing to find them together. And in that realization, there was a glimmer of hope, a fragile but enduring light in the darkness.

Liam's gaze softened slightly, but the shadows of his fears still lingered in his eyes. I could feel the tremble in his hands as I held them, and it mirrored the trembling of my own heart. His uncertainty was contagious, seeping into my own thoughts and amplifying my own fears. But I couldn't let it consume us. I needed to be strong, not just for me, but for both of us.

"I know it feels like you're standing on a precipice," I said quietly, my thumbs brushing gently over his knuckles. "But sometimes, the hardest part is just taking that first step into the unknown. And sometimes, it's worth the risk."

He blinked, as if my words were struggling to penetrate the fog of his anxiety. "But what if...what if this doesn't work out? What if

I'm left with nothing but a broken heart and a career that's fallen apart?"

I shook my head, my own emotions a whirlwind of determination and vulnerability. "That's always a possibility, Liam. But isn't it worth trying? Isn't it worth fighting for? If we don't take this chance, we might never know what could have been. We'll just be left with 'what ifs' and regrets."

He seemed to consider this, his face a canvas of conflicting emotions. There was a flicker of something in his eyes—a hint of hope, mingled with his fear. It was as though he was grappling with the idea that what we had might be worth more than the security he had built around himself. The notion of letting go of that control, even for a moment, was terrifying for him, but perhaps there was a sliver of belief starting to take root.

"I don't want to live a life full of regrets," he murmured, almost to himself. "I don't want to look back and wonder what could have happened if I had just taken a chance."

I nodded, feeling the weight of his words resonate with my own fears. "Neither do I," I said softly. "But if we're going to make this work, we have to face those fears together. We have to be willing to take the risk and see where it leads us. And even if things don't turn out the way we hope, at least we'll know we tried. We'll know that we fought for something real."

The silence that followed was filled with the echoes of our unspoken fears and hopes. Liam's shoulders seemed to relax slightly, and his grip on my hands softened. It was as if he was beginning to accept the idea that the fear of losing something might be outweighed by the possibility of gaining something truly meaningful.

"I just don't want to lose you," he said, his voice breaking slightly as he looked into my eyes with a sincerity that made my heart ache.

"I don't want to let go of something that's made me feel alive in a way I didn't think was possible."

My heart swelled at his confession, and I could feel tears threatening to spill. The vulnerability in his voice, the raw honesty of his words, made me realize just how deeply our connection had grown. We were standing on the edge of something profound, and despite the fear that lingered, there was also a powerful current of hope and love pulling us forward.

"You won't lose me," I said softly, my voice trembling with emotion. "Not if we don't let go. We've built something here that's worth fighting for. And even if the road ahead is uncertain, I'm willing to walk it with you."

His eyes searched mine for a moment longer before he finally nodded, a small, almost hesitant smile tugging at the corners of his lips. It was a tentative step toward hope, a fragile but significant acknowledgment that maybe, just maybe, we could find a way through the darkness together.

We stood there, holding each other's gaze, the silence between us now charged with a new kind of understanding. The road ahead was still unclear, and the fears that had plagued us weren't completely vanquished. But for the first time in what felt like an eternity, there was a glimmer of reassurance—a sense that whatever came next, we wouldn't be facing it alone.

And as we embraced, the weight of our fears seemed to lift just a little, replaced by the warmth of our shared resolve. We were still standing at the edge of the unknown, but we were no longer facing it as individuals. We were facing it together, and that was a step worth taking.

The days after Liam's confession were like a slow, sweet exhale, a lull in the chaos that had consumed us. We found ourselves slipping into a new rhythm, one that blended our work and our personal moments with a delicate ease. The tension that had been an ever-present shadow seemed to retreat, allowing us space to breathe and reconnect. It was as if, in the aftermath of our argument, we had both realized the importance of finding peace amid the storm.

Our routine shifted subtly. Mornings began with a shared breakfast, a stolen glance across the table as we sipped our coffee, the warmth of the drink mirroring the warmth growing between us. We would laugh over small things—Liam's attempts to decipher the menu in broken Italian or my failed attempts to master the art of ordering espresso without sounding like a tourist. These moments of normalcy, though seemingly mundane, became a source of comfort and joy.

In the afternoons, we would escape the confines of the villa and venture out into the town. The cobblestone streets seemed to hold a promise of adventure, leading us to hidden corners and charming cafes where time seemed to stand still. We wandered through markets bursting with colors, our hands occasionally brushing against each other, sending electric jolts up my arm. Each touch, though brief, felt like a secret pact between us, a silent affirmation that we were still very much connected despite the challenges we faced.

The beach became our sanctuary, a place where we could let our guard down completely. We'd walk along the shore, the cool sand squishing between our toes, the sound of waves crashing a soothing backdrop to our conversations. Liam would share stories from his past, moments of vulnerability that revealed his true self—his fears, his dreams, the sacrifices he had made. I listened, captivated, feeling each story etch itself into my heart. His words painted a portrait of a man who had fought fiercely for his place in the world, and I admired him more with each revelation.

There were also the quiet nights, when the stars stretched out above us like a vast, comforting blanket. We'd sit on the balcony, wrapped in each other's arms, sharing our dreams and aspirations.

We talked about what we hoped for after the shoot, the places we wanted to go, the things we wanted to achieve. For the first time, our conversations were not clouded by uncertainty or fear. Instead, they were filled with a hopeful anticipation of what the future might hold for us.

Yet, despite these moments of tranquility, the end of our time in Italy was an ever-present specter. It loomed over our days, a silent reminder that our perfect bubble would eventually burst. Each sunset seemed to carry with it a bittersweet edge, a reminder that our time together was finite. I would catch Liam's gaze sometimes, his eyes reflecting the same melancholy that I felt. We both knew that once we left this idyllic place, the real world, with all its complications and expectations, would rush back in.

The closer we got to the end of the shoot, the more I felt the weight of that ticking clock. We had built a sanctuary in Italy, a world where we could be ourselves without the constraints of our usual lives. But as the days dwindled, I couldn't help but wonder what would happen when we had to return to reality. Would the peace we had found here survive the transition back to our old lives?

In these moments of reflection, I clung to the hope that our time together had forged something strong and enduring. I believed that the connection we had built, the shared experiences and the deep conversations, could withstand the distance that would soon separate us. We had faced our fears and taken risks, and I was determined to believe that our bond was resilient enough to endure whatever came next.

Our final days in Italy were a whirlwind of mixed emotions—joy for the time we had shared and sadness for the impending farewell. We made a conscious effort to savor every moment, every kiss, every touch, knowing that these would be the memories we would carry with us. We danced in the streets, laughed under the stars, and embraced each day as if it were a precious gift.

As the end drew nearer, I found solace in the knowledge that, despite the challenges, we had managed to find a moment of peace together. It wasn't the end we had envisioned, but it was a beautiful chapter in our story, one that had deepened our connection and taught us the value of living in the present. And though the future remained uncertain, I held on to the hope that whatever came next would be shaped by the love and understanding we had nurtured in this magical place.

The days melted into a comfortable routine that felt both refreshing and bittersweet. Every morning, the sun seemed to rise with a newfound warmth, casting a golden hue over everything and making each moment feel like a precious gift. We discovered that these mornings were our sanctuary, a time to reconnect before the world intruded with its demands.

One morning, as we sipped our coffee on the balcony overlooking the sea, Liam's hand brushed against mine. It was a simple gesture, but it felt significant, a reminder of the tender intimacy we had shared in the midst of our struggles. We sat there in companionable silence, watching the sun stretch its fingers across the sky, the horizon awash with colors that seemed to echo the calm that had settled between us.

Our explorations of the town became our little adventures, each day offering something new and enchanting. We wandered through the narrow, winding streets, their charm undiminished by the bustle of tourists. We would lose ourselves among the quaint shops, each one a treasure trove of trinkets and local crafts. I reveled in the way Liam's eyes would light up when he found something he liked, his enthusiasm infectious. It was these moments, small and unremarkable in their simplicity, that carried a deeper significance for us, marking a time when everything felt right despite the ticking clock reminding us of our impending departure.

The beach, with its endless stretch of sand and surf, became our haven. We spent hours there, simply being present. Sometimes we'd lie side by side, soaking in the warmth of the sun, our hands intertwined, fingers tracing idle patterns on each other's skin. Other times, we'd walk along the water's edge, our footprints forming a temporary record of our journey together. The rhythm of the waves seemed to mirror the rhythm of our hearts, a soothing, almost hypnotic cadence that made everything else fall away.

One evening, we took a late-night walk through the town's quieter streets. The air was crisp and cool, carrying the faint scent of blooming jasmine. We talked about our lives back home, sharing fragments of our pasts that we hadn't yet revealed. Liam spoke of the sacrifices he'd made for his career, the late nights, the missed holidays, the constant pressure to succeed. I listened intently, my heart aching for the boy who had grown into the man before me. I told him about my own fears and dreams, the moments of doubt and triumph that had shaped me. It was a raw, honest exchange, one that deepened our connection and made the reality of our situation more poignant.

As the end of the shoot loomed closer, a subtle unease crept in despite our best efforts to live in the moment. The knowledge that our time together was limited hung like a shadow over our idyllic days. We both felt it, this creeping anxiety about what would happen when we left Italy. It was as if we were living in a beautiful dream that was bound to end, and no amount of savoring could change the inevitable reality.

One evening, as we sat on the beach watching the sun dip below the horizon, I turned to Liam, my heart heavy with unspoken fears. "Do you think we can make it work after this?" I asked, my voice barely audible above the sound of the waves. Liam's gaze was fixed on the horizon, his face illuminated by the last vestiges of daylight. For a long moment, he didn't answer, and I felt the weight of our unspoken worries pressing down on us.

Finally, he turned to me, his expression thoughtful and tender. "I don't know," he said slowly, his voice filled with a mix of hope and uncertainty. "But I do know that I don't want to leave here without knowing that we gave it everything we had."

His words, though tinged with doubt, were a balm to my anxious heart. We didn't have answers, didn't know what the future would hold, but we had each other in this moment. And as the darkness enveloped us, punctuated only by the distant twinkling of stars, I felt a sense of peace settle over me. Even with the uncertainty of what lay ahead, I knew that what we had now was real and precious. It was a solace I would hold onto as the clock continued its relentless countdown, savoring every fleeting moment we had left in this beautiful, ephemeral paradise.

We savored each sunset as though it were our last, letting the tranquility of the moment wash over us. One particular evening, we ventured to a secluded part of the beach, far from the familiar paths we had tread before. The sand here was soft and untouched, and the only sound was the gentle lapping of waves against the shore. We settled into a cozy spot, wrapped in a blanket we'd brought with us, the night air cool against our skin.

As Liam held me close, his arms encircling me with a warmth that seemed to transcend the chill of the evening, I felt a profound sense of peace. It was in these quiet moments that the weight of our situation seemed to lift, if only temporarily. We lay there, staring up at the starlit sky, talking in hushed tones about our dreams and what we hoped for the future.

Liam spoke of his aspirations, his voice filled with a mix of hope and uncertainty. He talked about wanting more than just a successful career, about finding a balance that would allow him to live a life he could be proud of, both personally and professionally. I listened, feeling a deep connection with his vulnerability. His dreams were no longer just abstract concepts; they were intricately tied to the person I had come to love.

In turn, I shared my own fears and hopes. I told him about the loneliness I had sometimes felt despite being surrounded by people, the yearning for something that felt real and lasting. We were both navigating uncharted waters, and it was in our honesty with each other that we found solace. There was no pretense between us, no masks to wear. We were simply two people laying bare their souls, and it felt both liberating and terrifying.

As the night wore on, the silence between us grew more comfortable, more profound. We watched the waves dance under the moonlight, the silver glow casting an ethereal shimmer on the water. Liam's fingers traced idle patterns on my arm, a tender gesture that spoke of his care and affection. The serenity of the moment wrapped around us, making the looming end of our time in Italy seem a little less daunting, if only for a while.

But as much as we tried to live in the moment, the reality of our situation was impossible to ignore. Every now and then, the thought of leaving this place, of returning to the chaos of our old lives, crept into our conversations and silences. It was a looming shadow that neither of us could escape. We had found a beautiful, fleeting peace in our time together, but we both knew that the world outside these moments was waiting for us to step back into it.

In those quiet nights and sunlit mornings, there was a bittersweet awareness that our time was limited. Every laugh we shared, every touch, every whispered promise felt like it was wrapped in a sense of urgency. The clock was ticking, and no matter how much we tried to freeze time, it kept moving forward, inexorably pulling us toward an uncertain future.

Despite the fears and uncertainties, we found a profound connection in our shared moments. The way Liam looked at me, the way he held me close, spoke of a deep-seated affection that transcended the immediate turmoil. It was clear that what we had was special, something worth fighting for, even if the path ahead was fraught with challenges.

As the days grew shorter and our time together began to slip away like sand through our fingers, we made a silent promise to ourselves and to each other. We would cherish the remaining moments, savoring the peace we had found amid the chaos. We would face the future with hope and determination, knowing that the bond we had forged in this beautiful place would carry us through whatever lay ahead.

The last day of the photoshoot dawned with a bittersweet clarity. The sun rose over the horizon, casting a soft, golden light that seemed to illuminate the finality of the day. There was a palpable sense of relief among the crew, their chatter and laughter echoing off the walls of the villa as they packed up equipment and sorted through last-minute details. For them, the end of the shoot was a chance to return to their normal lives, a welcomed pause in the whirlwind of travel and work.

But for Liam and me, the last day was something else entirely. The camaraderie of the crew contrasted sharply with the quiet tension that had settled between us. We had grown so accustomed to each other's presence, our days filled with shared glances and unspoken understanding. The thought of parting now seemed both impossible and inevitable. We busied ourselves with the tasks at hand, each movement charged with a silent acknowledgment that this was it.

As we worked side by side, the air was thick with unspoken words. The crew's excitement only highlighted the quiet storm raging within us. Every glance, every touch, seemed to carry the weight of our unvoiced fears and hopes. I caught myself stealing glances at Liam, trying to gauge his mood, his thoughts. He was a master of composure, but there was something in the way he moved, the way his eyes avoided mine, that spoke of his inner turmoil.

By evening, the villa was a flurry of activity. The final celebratory dinner was a loud, boisterous affair, filled with laughter and the clinking of glasses. Yet, amidst the revelry, Liam and I were drawn into a quieter, more personal space. We lingered at the edge of the gathering, our conversation turning from the usual light banter to something more profound. The joviality of the crew felt like a backdrop to our private farewell.

As the night wore on, the villa's lively atmosphere faded into a backdrop of hushed conversations and the soft glow of lanterns. Liam and I slipped away from the crowd, seeking solace in the privacy of the balcony where we had shared so many moments. The view was still breathtaking, the sprawling city lights twinkling below like stars come to rest. But tonight, the view felt different. The beauty of the scene seemed to mock the sadness we both felt.

We stood together in the quiet, the silence between us heavier than any words. I could feel the finality of the moment pressing down on me, a tangible weight in the cool night air. We both knew that this was our last night together in Italy, and the reality of what lay beyond seemed almost too painful to face.

I turned to Liam, my heart pounding with the question I had been dreading. "What happens now?" My voice was barely a whisper, as though speaking too loudly would shatter the fragile calm of our last moments together.

Liam's gaze dropped to the floor, his shoulders tensing slightly. His silence was louder than any words he might have spoken, a heavy acknowledgment of the uncertainty that loomed over us. I watched him struggle with his thoughts, the lines of his face etched with the same mix of fear and sorrow that I felt.

His fingers traced the edge of the railing, his touch almost reverent, as though he were trying to hold onto something tangible before it slipped away. When he finally looked up, his eyes met mine with a mixture of regret and resolve. "I don't know," he said, his voice strained. "I really don't know."

The truth of his words hit me like a cold wave. We had spent so much time trying to navigate the space between us, to find a way to make it work despite the odds. And now, as the end drew near, the reality of our situation seemed insurmountable. We had created a world for ourselves in those fleeting weeks, a sanctuary that was now on the brink of disappearing.

I took a deep breath, trying to steady my racing heart. "Maybe we don't need to have all the answers right now," I said softly, attempting to offer some measure of comfort. "Maybe we just need to focus on what we have, here and now."

Liam nodded slowly, his expression softening. "I wish things were different," he said, his voice filled with a quiet longing. "I wish we had more time."

We stood there in silence, the enormity of our situation sinking in. The future seemed as distant as the stars above, an uncharted territory we would have to face on our own. But for this moment, we clung to each other, finding solace in the shared sadness and the fleeting peace of our final night together.

As the night deepened and the villa fell into a serene quiet, we embraced the intimacy of the moment, knowing that whatever lay ahead, we had cherished the time we had spent together. It wasn't the end we had hoped for, but it was a poignant reminder of the love and connection we had built, even in the face of uncertainty.

As the last rays of sunlight faded behind the hills, Liam and I found ourselves alone, a small sanctuary away from the raucous celebration downstairs. The villa's balcony, which had once felt like a refuge, now seemed like the precipice of a new reality. The sky above was a canvas of darkening blues and purples, a stark contrast to the vibrant, carefree days we'd spent in Italy. The evening air was cool against my skin, but it did little to calm the tumult within me.

Liam leaned against the stone railing, his gaze lost in the distance, and for a moment, I wondered if he was searching for answers in the vast expanse before him. I felt a pang of sadness as I watched him, this man who had become so integral to my life in such a short span. His silence was deafening, a void that seemed to swallow up any remaining hope.

"I don't know what to say," he finally murmured, his voice rough, as though the words had been caught in his throat. He turned to face me, his eyes reflecting the last flickers of daylight. "I've been trying to find the right words, but they just... they escape me."

I took a deep breath, trying to steady the quake in my heart. "It's okay," I said softly. "I feel the same way. I keep thinking about what's next, how we're supposed to just go back to our lives as if these past weeks were just a dream."

He reached out, his hand brushing mine in a gesture both tender and urgent. The contact was a reminder of the depth of what we had shared, a fleeting connection that felt all too real. "I can't pretend I haven't thought about it," he admitted, his eyes searching mine for some semblance of clarity. "I'm scared of what happens when we leave this place. I've built my life around my career, around this facade I've created, and I don't know how to let it go."

His confession resonated with my own fears. I had been so focused on savoring each moment with him that I hadn't allowed myself to think about the future. Now, as the reality of our situation hit me with full force, the fear of returning to our separate lives was overwhelming.

"I don't want to lose what we have," I whispered, my voice trembling. "But I also don't want to go back to pretending. We've built something real here, something that means so much more than just a fling or a momentary escape."

Liam's eyes softened, and he stepped closer, closing the distance between us. "I know," he said, his voice barely above a whisper. "I keep thinking that maybe if I could just... I don't know, find a way to make it work, then maybe we could..."

I shook my head, feeling a mixture of frustration and sadness. "It's not just about making it work. It's about making a choice, about deciding what we want. And I don't think either of us can do that while we're still here, still wrapped up in this bubble of our own making."

The silence that followed was heavy, filled with the weight of our unspoken fears and hopes. Liam's hand lingered on mine, a silent promise that he didn't want to let go. "I want to try," he said finally, his voice filled with determination. "I want to find a way to make this real, to make us real."

I nodded, feeling a glimmer of hope amidst the uncertainty. "Then let's figure it out together," I said, squeezing his hand. "Let's not let this end with the shoot. Let's take a chance on what we've built."

We stood there for a long moment, holding onto each other as if the very act of touching could somehow bridge the gap between what we had and what was to come. The night was now fully upon us, the stars beginning to twinkle overhead. It was a symbol of both endings and beginnings, a reminder that even in the darkness, there could be light.

As the villa below continued to celebrate the end of the shoot, Liam and I remained in our private world, the future uncertain but the present filled with a quiet resolve. We knew that what lay ahead would be challenging, but for now, we chose to hold on to the hope that, somehow, we could make it work.

With a final, lingering kiss, we turned back to face the night, the uncertainty of the future overshadowed by the promise of what we could still build together.

The silence between us stretched like a heavy shroud, each passing second more suffocating than the last. Liam's eyes were fixed on the horizon, where the last remnants of daylight had succumbed to the creeping shadows of night. The night sky seemed endless, its vastness a poignant reminder of how small and fragile our situation felt.

I tried to grasp for words, but they were elusive, slipping through my fingers like sand. I had expected the end to be bittersweet, but I hadn't anticipated the depth of this particular sorrow. "I don't want this to end," I said, my voice barely above a whisper, as though speaking louder would somehow shatter the delicate balance we'd managed to hold onto.

Liam's gaze finally shifted back to me, his eyes reflecting a turmoil that mirrored my own. He stepped closer, the space between us shrinking until we were almost touching. "Neither do I," he said quietly. "But what are we supposed to do? How do we keep this—" he gestured vaguely between us, "—when we're back to our regular lives?"

The question hung in the air, a specter of uncertainty. I could see the anguish in his face, the way his brows furrowed as if trying to solve an impossible puzzle. My own heart ached at the thought of us returning to our separate lives, of losing the connection that had come to mean so much to both of us.

"Maybe we don't have to have all the answers," I suggested, feeling a flicker of hope amidst the despair. "Maybe it's enough to know that we've experienced something real, something worth holding onto."

He sighed, running a hand through his hair as if trying to brush away his doubts. "I'm scared," he admitted, his voice cracking with vulnerability. "Scared that once we leave here, everything we've built will just fall apart."

I reached out, placing my hand gently on his arm, feeling the warmth of his skin beneath my touch. "We can't predict the future," I said softly, trying to infuse my words with a sense of calm. "But we can choose to believe that what we have is worth fighting for. Even if it's hard, even if it's uncertain, we owe it to ourselves to try."

Liam's eyes searched mine, and for a moment, I felt as though we were standing on the edge of a precipice, looking out into an unknown expanse. The fear of the unknown was palpable, but so was the bond that had grown between us. In that moment, the gravity of our situation seemed to settle around us, and the only thing left was to confront it together.

He took a deep breath, as if summoning the strength to face whatever lay ahead. "You're right," he said, his voice steadier now. "We can't control everything, but we can make a choice. And I choose to hold onto this, to whatever we have, no matter where it takes us."

I nodded, a sense of relief mingled with the sadness that still lingered. It wasn't a perfect solution, but it was a start, a commitment to navigate the uncertainties together rather than succumb to them. The thought of leaving Italy was still painful, but there was a new resolve in Liam's words, a promise to face the future with courage rather than fear.

As we stood there, the cool night air brushing against our faces, I realized that this was the moment of truth. It wasn't about finding all the answers or knowing exactly how things would unfold. It was about choosing to embrace the journey, with all its unpredictability, and finding solace in the strength of our connection.

The villa behind us was quiet now, the celebration having long since ended. The world outside seemed to hold its breath, waiting for the dawn that would signal the end of our time here. But for now, in this fleeting moment of peace, I held onto Liam, savoring the closeness that had become so precious.

"Whatever happens," I said softly, "we'll face it together. We'll find our way."

He nodded, a faint smile touching his lips. "Together," he echoed, his voice filled with a determination that made my heart ache with both sadness and hope.

And as we stood there, wrapped in the quiet of the night, I clung to that promise, hoping that it would be enough to see us through the challenges ahead.

The morning we were set to leave, the villa seemed to hold its breath. The once vibrant, sunlit rooms now felt hollow, as if the joy and laughter we'd shared were only illusions, fading with the dawn. Every corner of the villa carried memories—our late-night conversations, the stolen kisses beneath the moonlight, the gentle promises whispered in the quiet. I felt the weight of those moments pressing down on me, even as the cold reality of departure loomed closer.

Liam and I moved about the house, gathering our things with a mechanical detachment that belied the storm of emotions brewing beneath the surface. The silence between us was thick, almost tangible, and it seemed to stretch endlessly as we waited for our respective cars to arrive. I watched him as he moved around, his shoulders slightly slumped, his gaze distant. I wanted to bridge the gap that had formed between us, but the words felt stuck in my throat, tangled with the same uncertainty that plagued him.

The moments ticked by with agonizing slowness, each second dragging out like a reminder of how close we had come to something beautiful and fragile. Just as I was beginning to lose hope, the quiet of the villa was broken by Liam's voice. It was low and strained, the kind of voice that revealed far more than he intended. "I don't want this to end," he said, turning to face me, his eyes reflecting a vulnerability that made my heart ache. "But I don't know how to make it work."

His confession hung in the air like a heavy fog, and I felt the sting of tears at the corners of my eyes. I took a step closer, my heart pounding in my chest. Reaching for his hand, I squeezed it tightly, trying to convey all the emotions that words couldn't capture. The touch of his skin against mine was a lifeline, grounding me in the midst of the chaos swirling around us.

"We'll figure it out," I whispered, my voice trembling but resolute. The promise felt fragile, like a delicate thread that might snap under too much pressure, but it was the only thing I could offer in that moment. His fingers tightened around mine, and for a brief second, we were both enveloped in a shared, unspoken hope. The uncertainty of the future seemed to waver, just slightly, as if our mutual resolve could shift the tides of fate.

The sound of engines rumbling outside brought us back to reality. Our cars were here the final signal that our time in Italy was drawing to a close. Liam's face was a mask of determination and sorrow as he glanced toward the door. He looked at me one last time, his gaze lingering with an intensity that made my heart ache.

"I don't want to say goodbye," he said quietly, almost to himself. I nodded, understanding all too well the depth of his feelings. There were so many things left unsaid, so many moments that we hadn't fully explored. The departure was more than just the end of a shoot; it felt like the end of a chapter in our lives, a chapter that had been filled with both passion and uncertainty.

As we stepped out of the villa and into the crisp morning air, the cool breeze was a stark contrast to the warmth we'd grown accustomed to. The reality of returning to our everyday lives was like a cold splash of water, jolting me awake from the dream-like state that Italy had wrapped around us. The cars were waiting, their engines idling impatiently, ready to whisk us away to our respective futures.

Liam and I shared a final, lingering look, a mix of regret and hope. There was no easy way to navigate the emotions swirling between us, no straightforward path to follow. All I knew was that the bond we'd formed was something significant, something worth fighting for, even if the fight was just beginning.

As we climbed into our separate vehicles, I glanced back at the villa one last time. The sun was climbing higher in the sky, casting long shadows across the landscape, and for a fleeting moment, I wished we could pause time and hold onto the serenity we'd found together. But time was relentless, and so was the journey ahead.

The engine roared to life, and as the car pulled away, I stole one last look at Liam, who stood at the edge of the driveway, his silhouette framed against the rising sun. The promise we had made lingered in the air, a fragile hope against the vast uncertainty of what lay ahead. And as Italy receded into the distance, I realized that this wasn't the end—it was just the beginning of something much more complicated, something that would require patience, courage, and a willingness to embrace the unknown.

The car engines roared to life, breaking the silence that had settled over us like a heavy, suffocating blanket. Liam and I exchanged one last, lingering glance before I climbed into my car. Every inch of the vehicle seemed to carry the weight of my unease. I sat there, staring out the window as the villa—our refuge—grew smaller in the distance. The landscape blurred, the scenery fading into a smudged canvas of greens and browns, as if the world itself was dissolving into the uncertainty we felt.

I tried to keep my thoughts focused on the promise I had made to Liam. We'd figure it out. But the enormity of that promise felt overwhelming. How could we bridge the gap that was now yawning between us, one that had widened with every unanswered question, every unsaid word? The excitement of our shared moments was overshadowed by the looming question of how to transition from the bubble we'd lived in to the reality waiting for us back home.

The car ride felt interminable. I was trapped in a maelstrom of emotions—each thought jostling for attention. What if this was just an ephemeral dream, something that seemed real only because of the magic of Italy? What if the real world was too harsh for what we had? Every curve in the road seemed to stretch the silence, pulling it tighter, until it was nearly unbearable.

When I finally reached my apartment, the familiarity of home seemed distant, almost foreign. The walls of my place, once comforting, now felt like the backdrop to a painful new reality. I dropped my bags, the thud of them hitting the floor echoing my sense of emptiness. The silence was louder here than it had been in the villa. The echo of Liam's voice, his confession, seemed to linger in the corners of the room, refusing to be forgotten.

I sank into the couch, staring at the empty space beside me where Liam's presence had been so vivid only days before. The memory of his touch, his voice, filled the void, but it did little to soothe the ache of his absence. My phone buzzed, a notification flashing across the screen. I almost ignored it, but something compelled me to check. It was a message from Liam.

"I'm sorry," it began, the words striking me like a sudden gust of wind. "I've been thinking all day, and I can't stop replaying our last conversation. I know I need to be honest with you, even if it's hard."

I swallowed hard, my fingers trembling as I typed a reply. "What are you thinking?" I sent the message, my heart racing. The minutes ticked by with excruciating slowness, each second stretching into what felt like an eternity. Finally, his response came through.

"I'm scared," he admitted. "I want this—us—to work more than anything. But I'm terrified of what happens next. I don't know how to navigate this, how to make it last. I don't want to lose what we have, but I also don't want to set us up for disappointment."

His words mirrored the fears that had been plaguing me since we left Italy. It was as if he had reached across the miles that separated us to voice the very thoughts that had been swirling in my mind. I took a deep breath, trying to find the right words to reassure him, to offer some semblance of hope amidst the uncertainty.

"We both have fears," I wrote back, trying to convey my feelings with as much honesty as he had shown. "But I think we owe it to ourselves to try, to face the unknown together. We can't predict the future, but we can decide to be brave enough to embrace it, whatever it may bring."

There was a long pause before he replied. "You're right. I want to try. I don't want to let fear dictate our future. I just need to figure out how to do this, how to make sure we don't lose each other."

The exchange was a small comfort, a glimmer of understanding in the midst of our fears. It didn't solve everything, but it was a start. It was a reminder that despite the physical distance, we still shared a connection that was worth fighting for.

As I lay in bed that night, the promise I had made to Liam echoed in my mind. This wasn't the end—it was the beginning of something more complex and uncertain. We had faced the beauty of Italy together, and now we had to face the challenges of reality. It wouldn't be easy, but maybe, just maybe, we had enough courage and commitment to see it through. And as sleep finally claimed me, I held on to the hope that the future might hold more for us than either of us dared to dream.

The hum of the city seemed different as I returned to it, each sound amplified by the weight of the past few weeks. My apartment, once a sanctuary, now felt like a cage. Every corner, every object seemed to bear witness to the absence of Liam. I slumped onto the couch, staring blankly at the mess of unpacked bags around me. The ache of parting was so fresh that it felt as if it were still lingering in the air, mingling with the scent of the Italian nights that now felt like distant memories.

My phone buzzed once more, pulling me out of my reverie. The screen illuminated with Liam's name. I hesitated, the fluttering anticipation battling with a rising dread. I took a deep breath and opened the message. It was a simple text, yet the weight of its words was profound.

"I'm sorry for not being more clear. I don't know what comes next, but I can't stop thinking about you. I hope we can talk soon."

A mix of relief and anxiety washed over me. His words were a balm to the raw, exposed nerves that had been frayed by our departure. Yet, they also confirmed my fears: the uncertainty wasn't just in my mind; it was real, a palpable force that could not be ignored. I typed a quick response, my fingers trembling as I tried to find the right balance between hope and practicality.

"Me too. I don't know what happens next either, but I want to talk. Let's figure this out."

I pressed send, my heart racing as if the act of sending the message would somehow make a difference. As I set the phone aside, I tried to focus on the space around me, on the life that awaited me outside of the bubble we'd created in Italy. The silence of my apartment seemed to swallow me whole, and I found myself longing for the gentle chaos of the villa, the soft laughter and unspoken understanding that had threaded through our days there.

The days that followed were a blur of routine and restlessness. The rhythm of my old life was a stark contrast to the vibrancy of our shared moments. I immersed myself in work, burying myself in tasks to avoid the crushing silence that seemed to stretch endlessly in the spaces Liam used to fill. I found myself replaying our last moments together over and over, searching for answers in his gaze, his touch, his words.

The tension between us, even through our messages, was palpable. Our conversations were a dance around the heart of the matter—our futures, our fears, and what came next. Each message felt like a lifeline and a reminder of the distance that now lay between us. We both avoided discussing the elephant in the room, our professional commitments that would soon pull us in different directions.

One evening, as I sat at my kitchen table, the mundane task of sorting through mail felt surreal. The world outside seemed to move on while I was stuck in a loop of waiting, hoping for some sign that would lead me to a clear path forward. The phone buzzed again, and this time, the message from Liam was longer, more detailed.

"I've been thinking a lot about what we said, about the future. I know I've been distant, and I'm sorry for that. I want to be honest with you about how I feel and what I want. I hope you can understand that this isn't easy for me. Let's meet and talk."

My heart leapt at the prospect of seeing him again, of bridging the gap that had formed between us. I could feel a glimmer of hope piercing through the fog of uncertainty. It wasn't a solution, but it was a step towards one. I replied with a mix of eagerness and caution, agreeing to meet him as soon as possible.

The anticipation of our meeting was a bittersweet comfort, a distraction from the monotony of my day-to-day life. As the days ticked by, I clung to the idea of us finding a way forward, even as the reality of our separation loomed large. The knowledge that Liam was just as eager to talk, to figure things out, was a small but significant solace.

Finally, the day arrived when we would see each other again. I was a bundle of nerves and hope, preparing myself for whatever came next. The weight of our last moments together hung heavy, but the promise of confronting our reality, together, gave me a sense of cautious optimism. This was not the end; it was a new beginning, fraught with challenges but full of potential.

As I approached the meeting spot, the reality of facing Liam again brought a flood of emotions. I took a deep breath, ready to confront the uncertainties head-on. The beginning of our new chapter awaited us, and despite the fear and doubt, I held on to the hope that we could navigate through it together.

Returning to New York felt like being pulled back into a world that no longer fit the person I had become. The city's frenetic pulse, the cacophony of honking taxis and distant sirens, seemed to mock the serene moments I had experienced in Italy. I had traded sun-drenched alleys and the gentle rhythm of the Mediterranean for the harsh glare of neon lights and the relentless rush of the city. Each day, I walked through the streets feeling like an outsider, grappling with the dissonance between my former life and the new, more vibrant self I had discovered with Liam.

My apartment, once a cozy refuge, now felt like a cavernous shell. The familiar space was stifling, haunted by echoes of our laughter and whispered conversations. I found myself reaching for the phone more often than usual, hoping for a text or a call from Liam, but the messages we exchanged grew less frequent. When they did come, they were brief and polite, as if we were both trying to hold onto something that was slipping through our fingers. The intimacy we had shared seemed so distant now, and I struggled to reconcile the vibrant life I had in Italy with the mundane routine of New York.

Work was supposed to be my escape, a way to distract myself from the emptiness. I threw myself into new projects, eagerly accepting assignments that came my way. My camera, once a tool of passion and discovery, became a reminder of everything I was trying to forget. Each click of the shutter felt like a stab in the dark, capturing moments that seemed so trivial compared to the intensity of what I had experienced with Liam. The photos I took were lifeless, lacking the magic I had felt in the Italian landscapes, where every frame seemed infused with the warmth of our shared connection.

Despite my efforts to immerse myself in work, I found it increasingly difficult to concentrate. The city's vibrancy was overshadowed by a persistent sense of loss. The high-energy, fast-paced rhythm of New York was a harsh contrast to the slow, deliberate pace of our time together. The memories of Italy were vivid and relentless, intruding on every moment of my day. I would catch myself daydreaming of our walks along the coast, the way Liam's laughter had filled the air, or the way he had looked at me when he thought I wasn't watching. Those moments were like a movie playing in my head, endlessly replaying and reminding me of a world I longed to return to.

I began to doubt whether our connection was strong enough to withstand the separation. The weeks turned into months, and as the seasons changed, so did the nature of our conversations. What had once been deep and meaningful was now reduced to polite inquiries about each other's well-being. The emotional intimacy we had shared seemed to be fading, replaced by the casual updates of two people trying to stay connected despite the growing distance. Each time we spoke, I could sense the struggle behind his words, the effort to maintain a semblance of the closeness we once had.

One evening, after a particularly grueling day at work, I found myself standing by the window, staring out at the city skyline. The lights of New York shimmered like distant stars, but they offered no comfort. My reflection in the glass looked tired and worn, a stark contrast to the vibrant image of myself I had glimpsed in Italy. I wondered if this was how it was supposed to be—if the excitement of our brief but intense connection was destined to dissolve into the routine of everyday life.

I picked up my phone and considered calling Liam, but hesitation held me back. The thought of confronting the growing chasm between us was daunting, and I wasn't sure how to bridge it. The fear of what the conversation might reveal kept me from reaching out. What if our connection was not as strong as I had hoped? What if our time together in Italy was nothing more than a beautiful interlude in our lives, destined to remain a cherished memory rather than the beginning of something lasting?

As I stood there, the weight of the unanswered questions settled heavily on my shoulders. The distance between us seemed to be growing with each passing day, and the hope of finding a way to bridge that gap felt increasingly elusive. In the quiet of my apartment, I was left to grapple with the reality of our situation, knowing that finding a path forward would require more than just holding onto memories. It would require confronting the truth of what we had become and what we were willing to do to keep it alive.

In the silence of my apartment, I began to question everything that had happened. I would sit by the window, watching the city move in its relentless rhythm while I felt stagnant and adrift. The initial excitement of returning to my old life was quickly overshadowed by an unshakable melancholy. The streets of New York, which had once been vibrant and full of promise, now seemed harsh and unforgiving. Every corner, every building, felt like a reminder of what I had left behind and what I was losing.

I tried to find solace in familiar routines, but nothing seemed to fit. The cafes I used to frequent felt alien, and my favorite bookstore, once a sanctuary, now seemed a place of lonely reflection. Conversations with friends felt superficial, and my attempts to reintegrate into my social circle only highlighted how much had changed. I was no longer the person who had walked these streets a few months ago. Italy had left an indelible mark on me, one that New York could not easily erase.

The sporadic messages and brief phone calls with Liam did little to fill the void. We would talk about the mundane details of our daily lives, but the deeper conversations we used to share were missing. It felt as though we were both holding back, trying to avoid the topic of what had happened between us and where we might go from here. The promises we made to stay in touch seemed increasingly hollow as the days wore on.

In an attempt to regain some sense of normalcy, I threw myself into my work with renewed fervor. I took on new assignments, started new projects, and tried to immerse myself in the creative process. Yet, every time I picked up my camera, I was haunted by memories of our time together. The lens, which once felt like an extension of my vision, now felt like a barrier between me and the world I was trying to capture. The images I took were technically perfect but emotionally vacant. I missed the connection I had felt while photographing Italy, and no amount of professional success could replace the personal fulfillment I had experienced.

One evening, while sifting through photos from the shoot, I came across a series of images I had taken of Liam. They were candid shots, stolen moments that captured the essence of who he was—his laughter, the way he looked when he was deep in thought, the warmth of his presence. As I stared at these images, the ache of missing him became almost unbearable. The photographs were a testament to the bond we had shared, a bond that seemed both precious and elusive now that we were apart.

The more I reflected on our time together, the more I realized that the connection we had was something rare and special. It wasn't just about the romance or the physical attraction; it was about a deep, emotional resonance that I had never felt before. I had thought that returning to New York would help me move on, but instead, it made me question the choices I had made and the future we had envisioned.

As the days turned into weeks, the reality of our separation began to sink in. I found myself grappling with a sense of loss that was both profound and disorienting. The excitement of starting a new chapter in my life felt overshadowed by the uncertainty of where Liam and I stood. We had both hoped that time and distance would provide clarity, but instead, it seemed to amplify the distance between us.

I tried to focus on the positives—my career was thriving, and I had opportunities that I had always dreamed of. Yet, these achievements felt hollow without Liam to share them with. The sense of accomplishment was marred by the emptiness that came from missing someone who had become so integral to my life.

In the quiet moments of reflection, I began to understand that this period of separation was not just about adjusting to a new reality; it was about facing the truth of what I truly wanted. The lessons I had learned in Italy had changed me in ways I hadn't fully grasped before. The connection with Liam was something that I couldn't easily dismiss or replace, and the future seemed uncertain as I grappled with the choices that lay ahead.

The city moved on around me, oblivious to the internal struggle I was facing. I walked through its streets, capturing images and living my life, but a part of me remained tethered to the memories of Italy and the unresolved feelings I had for Liam. As I navigated this new chapter, I knew that whatever came next would require courage, honesty, and a willingness to confront the complexities of love and distance.

I spent evenings curled up on my couch, staring blankly at the television, which seemed to blur together in a haze of colors and sounds that failed to captivate me. My thoughts would drift back to Italy, to Liam, and the moments we had shared. The laughter, the quiet talks, the way his eyes would light up when he spoke about his passions—it all felt like a beautiful dream that had slipped through my fingers.

On one particularly grey afternoon, I decided to visit a small art gallery in SoHo. I had been avoiding places that reminded me of our time together, but something compelled me to go. As I walked through the gallery, each piece of art seemed to echo my feelings of confusion and loss. I found myself standing in front of a large abstract painting, its swirling colors a chaotic representation of the storm inside me. I could almost feel the artist's desperation, a longing for something just out of reach, much like my own.

Returning home, I noticed a letter slipped under my door. The envelope was unmarked, the handwriting unfamiliar. Curiosity gnawed at me as I opened it. Inside was a single photograph, one I had never seen before—a candid shot of Liam and me, laughing together in a sunlit piazza. The image was so vivid, so full of life, that it nearly took my breath away. There was no note, no explanation, just that photo—a simple, poignant reminder of everything that had been and everything I was trying to hold onto.

The photograph sat on my desk, a constant reminder of the distance between us. I began to wonder if our connection had been a fleeting moment, a beautiful interlude in a larger, more complicated story. I questioned whether it was possible to bridge the gap that had formed between us, or if we were destined to remain as distant as the continents that separated us.

I kept thinking about the last conversation we had before leaving Italy. The uncertainty in Liam's voice, the way he struggled to find the right words—it was as if he was trying to articulate the very essence of our situation, and failing. I understood his fears, his hesitation, but it didn't make it any easier to accept. I wanted to believe that our bond was strong enough to survive the distance, but the silence that followed our departure made me doubt everything.

One evening, after a particularly frustrating day at work, I found myself standing on my balcony, watching the city lights flicker in the distance. The view was a stark contrast to the rolling hills and ancient streets of Italy, yet there was a strange comfort in the familiarity of the skyline. As I leaned against the railing, my phone buzzed with a new message from Liam.

My heart raced as I opened the message. It was brief, just a few lines, but it carried a weight that felt both heavy and hopeful. He talked about how he missed me, how the city felt emptier without me by his side. The message ended with a simple question: "How are you holding up?"

For a moment, I was overwhelmed by a wave of relief and sadness. Relief that he still thought of me, that he was reaching out despite the distance. Sadness because the message was a stark reminder of the reality we faced. We were separated by more than just miles; we were separated by our lives, our routines, and the unspoken fears that loomed over us.

I typed out a response, taking my time to find the right words. I told him that I missed him too, that the city felt colder without him. I shared a little about how work had been going and how I was trying to adjust to the new normal. I didn't mention the photograph or the weight of our unspoken concerns. I wanted to keep the message light, hopeful, even if I wasn't entirely sure how to feel.

As I hit send, I felt a strange mix of hope and resignation. Maybe this was our new reality—a series of messages and fleeting connections, each one a small attempt to bridge the gap between us. Maybe this was the beginning of a different kind of relationship, one that required patience and understanding, and a willingness to navigate the uncertainty together.

As the city lights continued to twinkle in the distance, I took a deep breath and allowed myself to hope. Maybe, just maybe, this wasn't the end of our story, but rather a new chapter—one that would require effort, commitment, and a lot of heart. I closed my eyes and let the quiet of the night wash over me, finding solace in the possibility that, despite everything, we could still find a way to make it work.

The days seemed to stretch endlessly, each one blending into the next with an unforgiving monotony. My frustration was a constant companion, gnawing at the edges of my patience. I replayed every conversation with Liam in my mind, searching for clues, for signs that maybe, just maybe, things weren't as bleak as they seemed. But each time I called, or sent a message, the responses were clipped, as if he were speaking through a veil of disconnection that only seemed to grow thicker with each passing day.

His career had always been demanding, but I had expected that the connection we forged in Italy would be a beacon through the fog of his busy life. Instead, it felt like a distant memory, something we once clung to but now struggled to maintain. The moments of shared laughter, the long conversations where we bared our souls, seemed so far away. The vulnerability that had been our strength now felt like a chasm between us, filled with unspoken doubts and a growing silence.

Each call was a brief exchange of pleasantries that left me feeling more alone than before. The way he spoke, the tone of his voice, it was all too calculated, too restrained. I tried to understand, to rationalize his distance as a byproduct of his hectic schedule, but it didn't make the sting of rejection any easier to bear. I wondered if I had been nothing more than a distraction for him—a temporary escape from the pressures of his life, now replaced by the relentless demands of his career.

On those days when the silence became unbearable, I found myself wandering the city, hoping that the familiar streets would offer some solace. I would lose myself in the crowded parks, the bustling cafes, trying to find a semblance of normalcy amidst the chaos of my thoughts. Each corner I turned, each street I walked down, seemed to echo the emptiness I felt inside.

One particularly gray afternoon, I found myself sitting on a bench in Central Park, watching the leaves fall from the trees in a slow, deliberate dance. The chill in the air mirrored the coldness that had seeped into my heart. I took out my phone, staring at the screen with a mixture of hope and despair. Should I call him again? Should I send another message? The cycle of anticipation and disappointment had become a relentless pattern, each interaction leaving me feeling more disconnected.

I ran my fingers over the photograph that had been left under my door, the one of Liam and me in Italy. It was a stark reminder of what we had, and how quickly it had slipped away. I had hoped it would bring me comfort, but instead, it deepened my longing and frustration. The image was filled with joy and light, and yet, it felt like a cruel joke against the backdrop of my present reality.

The more I tried to reach out, the more I felt like I was pushing him further away. It was as if the very effort to hold onto something was driving him away. The space between us grew, and with it, my fear that I was losing him completely. I questioned whether my feelings for him had been a temporary infatuation, a romantic illusion created by the magic of Italy, or if there was a genuine connection that we had somehow let slip through our fingers.

Every attempt to rekindle the spark felt like it was met with indifference or confusion. The ease with which we had once connected seemed like a distant dream, replaced by a new reality where every word had to be measured, every sentiment dissected. I missed the comfort of knowing where I stood with him, the way his presence made me feel grounded.

The days continued to drift by, each one adding weight to the burden I carried. I tried to focus on my work, immersing myself in projects that demanded my attention. But even as I threw myself into my career, I couldn't escape the constant reminder of what I had lost.

Each photograph I took seemed to capture only a fraction of the joy and connection I once felt.

The struggle to hold on became a daily battle, one where I questioned whether the effort was worth the pain. Every day without Liam felt like a test of my resolve, my ability to endure the uncertainty that lay ahead. It was a struggle not just to keep our connection alive, but to keep my own sense of self intact amidst the chaos of my emotions.

I wanted to believe that this was just a rough patch, that we would find our way back to each other. But as the weeks stretched on, I couldn't shake the feeling that something precious was slipping away, and I wasn't sure if there was anything I could do to stop it. The only thing I could cling to was the hope that, somehow, amidst the confusion and distance, we would find our way back to the place where everything had once felt so right.

I spent the better part of my days lost in a fog of uncertainty, trying to fill the emptiness with work and distractions. But even the most engaging projects couldn't erase the persistent ache that lingered whenever I thought of Liam. Each photo I took, each image I edited, seemed to whisper reminders of what once was—a connection that felt genuine, a bond that seemed unbreakable.

Every morning, I woke with a glimmer of hope that today might be different, that today might bring a breakthrough in our communication. But the reality was often disappointing. I'd check my phone obsessively, my heart skipping a beat with every notification, only to be let down by a brief text or a missed call. It was as if we were both trapped in a cycle of half-hearted attempts, struggling to hold onto something that was slipping through our fingers.

The silence between us grew heavier, each missed call and unanswered text contributing to a growing chasm. I tried to remind myself that his career was demanding, that he was under immense pressure, but it did little to soothe the ache of his absence. The vulnerability we had once shared seemed like a distant dream, replaced by a façade of politeness and formality that felt foreign and uncomfortable.

One evening, as I stared out of my apartment window at the city lights flickering in the distance, I felt the weight of my own emotions pressing down on me. I had spent so much time trying to understand him, trying to bridge the gap between us, that I had neglected to address my own needs and fears. The emptiness I felt wasn't just about his absence; it was also about the uncertainty of where we stood, of whether we were moving towards something or simply drifting apart.

In a moment of desperation, I decided to reach out to him once more. My fingers hovered over the keyboard as I typed out a message, each word carefully chosen, each sentence a reflection of my longing for clarity. I wanted to ask him about us, to understand what he felt and what he wanted. But as I read over the message, I hesitated. Was I being too pushy? Was I overstepping boundaries? I didn't want to force him into a conversation he wasn't ready for, but the silence was becoming unbearable.

Eventually, I hit send, the message disappearing into the ether. I paced my apartment, the minutes stretching into hours as I awaited his response. The uncertainty was almost too much to bear, each passing moment amplifying my anxiety. I wanted to believe that he would reply, that we could find a way to make things work, but the fear of rejection and disappointment loomed large.

When the notification finally came, I almost didn't want to look. My heart raced as I opened the message, only to be met with a brief reply that offered little comfort. He was busy, he missed me, but he didn't know how to balance everything. The words were familiar, echoes of past conversations that hadn't led to any real resolution. I read and reread his response, trying to extract some meaning, some hope from his words. But all I found was more of the same—more ambiguity, more distance.

As the days continued to blur together, I tried to focus on the small things that brought me joy, the moments of connection with friends, the satisfaction of completing a project. But even these distractions couldn't fully erase the sense of longing that remained. I couldn't help but wonder if we were merely holding onto a memory, a fleeting moment of happiness that had once seemed real but was now drifting away.

I found myself grappling with the reality of our situation, trying to come to terms with the possibility that maybe, just maybe, we weren't meant to hold on to what we had. The pain of letting go was almost too much to bear, but the weight of uncertainty was becoming unbearable. In my heart, I still hoped for a resolution, for a chance to rebuild what we had, but the path forward seemed increasingly unclear.

In those quiet moments of reflection, I began to realize that while I couldn't force him to be present, I could choose how to navigate my own journey. The struggle to hold on was taking a toll on me, and perhaps it was time to focus on finding my own peace amidst the chaos.

As the days wore on, the silence between us began to weigh heavily. Each unreturned call and missed message felt like a fresh wound, reopening the insecurities I had tried so hard to keep at bay. I found myself replaying our last conversation over and over in my mind, searching for clues or signs that might explain why things had changed so abruptly. Had I done something wrong? Had I somehow become an afterthought in his whirlwind of responsibilities?

The more I thought about it, the more I questioned the reality of our connection. What had started so passionately seemed to be dissolving into an echo of what it once was. It was as if the vibrant, thrilling colors of our relationship had faded into muted tones, and I was left clinging to the remnants of something that felt increasingly distant.

One particularly lonely afternoon, as I sifted through old photographs from our time in Italy, a pang of nostalgia hit me hard. The laughter, the intimate conversations, the way he looked at me with that intensity—it all felt like a dream now, something too beautiful to be real. I could almost hear his voice in my head, his words full of hope and promise. But that voice was now replaced by a void, a silence that spoke louder than any words ever could.

Desperate for some clarity, I decided to make an unannounced visit to a café we used to frequent. It was a place that held so many memories for us—where we had shared countless conversations and stolen glances. I hoped that being there might somehow provide answers or at least offer some comfort amidst the confusion. As I walked through the door, the familiar aroma of coffee and pastries wrapped around me, a bittersweet reminder of those simpler times.

I settled into a corner booth, my usual spot, and ordered a cappuccino. The café was bustling with life, the chatter of customers blending into a soothing background hum. I watched as people went about their day, wondering if they too had moments of heartache and longing that they kept hidden beneath their everyday smiles. It was in this space, surrounded by memories and the noise of normalcy, that I felt the sharpest pang of loneliness.

As I sipped my coffee, my phone buzzed, and my heart skipped a beat. It was a message from Liam. My hands trembled slightly as I opened it, hoping for something reassuring. But the message was brief, an apology for not being in touch and an explanation about work commitments. It was polite and respectful but lacked the warmth and depth that once defined our conversations.

I felt a rush of frustration and sadness. Was this all we had left? A series of polite exchanges that barely scratched the surface of what we had shared? I wanted to respond, to pour out my heart and tell him how much I missed him, but the words seemed to catch in my throat. I was caught between wanting to reach out and fearing that doing so would push him further away.

The truth was, I didn't know how to handle this new reality. I had been so certain of what we had in Italy, so sure that it was something worth fighting for. But now, the lines between us were blurred, and I struggled to see a path forward. I had to come to terms with the possibility that maybe, despite our best efforts, some things weren't meant to last.

As the afternoon sun began to set, casting long shadows across the café, I realized that I needed to take a step back and reassess what I wanted. I couldn't force a connection that seemed to be slipping away, and I couldn't ignore my own needs and emotions in the process. I had to find a way to move forward, whether that meant holding on with whatever strength I had left or letting go and embracing whatever came next.

With a heavy heart, I finished my coffee and stood up, leaving a generous tip for the barista. As I walked out of the café, I took a deep breath, trying to find some semblance of peace amidst the uncertainty. The city seemed to have returned to its usual pace, but for me, the days ahead were anything but clear. All I knew was that I had to navigate this new chapter of my life with honesty and courage, no matter how daunting it might seem.

The distance between us had become more than just miles; it had crept into every corner of my mind, filling it with shadows of doubt and worry. It was a gnawing, relentless presence, the kind that kept me awake at night, turning over every possible scenario, every missed call, every unanswered text. It felt like I was trapped in a fog, the clarity of our once vibrant connection now obscured by a haze of uncertainty and fear.

One night, as I lay in bed staring at the ceiling, the quiet of my apartment seemed to amplify the silence that had grown between us. Liam's absence was a palpable weight, pressing down on me and making every breath feel heavy. I had tried to be patient, to hold onto the hope that things would improve, but the persistent emptiness gnawed at me with a cruel persistence.

I found myself replaying our last conversation, dissecting each word, each pause, searching for the moment where things had started to unravel. "We'll figure it out," I had said, trying to sound more confident than I felt. But the words now felt hollow, a promise that seemed increasingly unattainable. My heart ached with the realization that despite our best intentions, we were drifting apart. It was as though the more we tried to bridge the gap, the wider it seemed to grow.

My friends, bless their hearts, did their best to comfort me. They spoke of the challenges of long-distance relationships, the struggles and sacrifices involved. They told me that it was normal to feel this way, that it was part of the process. But their words, though well-meaning, only seemed to highlight the void that was growing between Liam and me. They didn't know the way his silence felt like a chasm that I couldn't cross, the way each day without him seemed to deepen the divide.

I tried to stay busy, to immerse myself in work and distractions. I threw myself into new projects with a fervor that bordered on obsession, hoping that if I could just keep my mind occupied, I might forget the gnawing worry that had taken root. But every time I picked up my camera, every time I clicked the shutter, I was reminded of him—the way he had looked through my lens, the way his smile had lit up a room. The absence of those moments was a constant reminder of what I was missing.

It was in the midst of this struggle that I found myself seeking solace in the mundane. I took long walks through the city, trying to clear my mind, to find some semblance of peace amidst the chaos. But even the familiar streets of New York felt alien and cold without

Liam by my side. I had once found comfort in the city's energy, but now it seemed to mock me with its indifference, a stark contrast to the warmth I had experienced in Italy.

One particularly rainy evening, I found myself in a small café that had become a refuge of sorts. The rain tapped against the windowpane in a rhythmic pattern, a soothing backdrop to my swirling thoughts. I sipped on a steaming cup of tea, hoping that the simple act of taking a break might offer some clarity. But the more I tried to find answers, the more elusive they seemed. The café's warmth did little to thaw the chill that had settled over my heart.

In the midst of my reflections, my phone buzzed with a new message. My heart leaped, a fleeting hope that perhaps Liam had reached out with some words of reassurance. I fumbled to unlock the screen, but as I read the message, the hope that had momentarily flared was quickly extinguished. It was another polite but distant text, an update on his busy schedule, filled with apologies for not being able to talk more. The words, though courteous, felt like a reminder of the distance that had grown between us.

As I sat there, staring at the message, I couldn't help but feel a profound sense of disconnection. It was as though our once vivid and intimate moments had been reduced to mere echoes, reverberating through the void that now separated us. I longed for the days when our conversations had flowed effortlessly, when the connection between us had felt unbreakable.

The doubts that had been simmering beneath the surface now bubbled up with full force. Was I clinging to something that was no longer real? Had the dream we had built together become a fragile illusion, unable to withstand the pressures of reality? I struggled with these thoughts, feeling both a sense of betrayal and a deep, aching sorrow. It was as though the more I tried to hold on, the more it slipped through my fingers, leaving me with nothing but a hollow sense of loss.

In that moment, I realized that I was at a crossroads. The path ahead seemed uncertain, filled with potential pitfalls and heartache. I had to decide whether to keep fighting for something that felt increasingly out of reach or to let go and try to move forward. The choice was daunting, and the fear of making the wrong decision paralyzed me. But deep down, I knew that the only way to find clarity was to confront these doubts head-on and make a decision based on what was best for both of us, even if it meant facing the possibility of letting go.

The more I thought about it, the harder it became to hold on to hope. The gap between us felt less like a mere physical separation and more like a vast, unbridgeable chasm. Each passing day seemed to stretch longer than the one before, as if time itself were conspiring against us. I couldn't remember the last time our conversations had flowed effortlessly, when each exchange felt like a piece of a puzzle falling perfectly into place. Now, they felt like forced attempts to grasp at something that was slipping further from our reach.

My apartment, once a sanctuary of creativity and inspiration, now felt suffocating. I wandered through it like a ghost, my mind constantly wandering back to Italy. I could almost feel the warmth of the sun on my skin, the softness of Liam's touch. I would see his face in fleeting memories, in the corners of my photographs, and it would pierce my heart with a sharp pang of nostalgia. It was as if the more I tried to move forward, the more I was pulled back to that moment in time when everything felt so right, so easy.

Despite my best efforts to stay positive, I found myself spiraling deeper into doubt. Every missed call, every delayed text seemed to build a wall between us, brick by brick. I tried to tell myself that this was normal, that relationships faced these hurdles, but the rational part of my mind felt increasingly distant. My heart, on the other hand, was in turmoil, caught between the desire to fight for what we had and the fear of being hurt by what might never be.

One evening, after another disheartening attempt to reach Liam, I found myself sitting alone in a small café, nursing a cup of lukewarm coffee. The café was bustling with the usual evening crowd, but the noise seemed muffled to me. I felt detached from the world around me, as though I were watching life from behind a thick glass pane. My thoughts were a tangled mess of hope and despair, and the barista's cheerful chatter only served to highlight my isolation.

I pulled out my phone and stared at it, willing it to ring, to show me a message from him, but the screen remained stubbornly blank. I had sent another message earlier in the day, hoping that maybe, just maybe, this time I'd get a response that would clear the fog of uncertainty hanging over me. I kept checking, but the silence was deafening.

As I sat there, I couldn't help but think about the reality of our situation. Liam was living a life so different from mine—one filled with constant movement, endless commitments, and a world that seemed so far removed from the quiet moments we had shared. I wondered if he had found a way to adapt, to live without the presence of our moments together, while I struggled to understand how to move forward without him.

The more I reflected, the more I questioned whether I was being realistic or simply clinging to a memory of something that had been beautiful but was no longer feasible. It was a cruel twist of fate that the very thing that had brought us together was now the thing threatening to pull us apart. The connection that had once felt so tangible now felt like a mere echo, a whisper of something that had been real but was now fading away.

I closed my eyes and took a deep breath, trying to steady the storm within me. The café was warm and filled with the comforting aroma of coffee, but the warmth did little to thaw the chill of doubt that had settled over me. I wanted to believe that there was still a chance for us, that this was just a rough patch that we could overcome. But every moment of silence, every unanswered question seemed to chip away at the faith I had once held so firmly.

I longed for a sign, a clear indication that what we had was worth fighting for. Yet, as I sat in that bustling café, surrounded by the noise of everyday life, I felt more isolated than ever. The future was an uncertain shadow, stretching out before me, and I was left grappling with the painful realization that perhaps the hardest part of love was not the falling but the trying to hold on when it felt like it was slipping through your fingers.

I found myself sinking deeper into the murky waters of doubt, each day blurring into the next in a haze of confusion. The apartment, once filled with the energy of new beginnings and the promise of something profound, now seemed like a shell of its former self. My studio, where I had once poured my heart into my work, now felt like a space I was merely occupying. The joy I had found in my photography was now overshadowed by a persistent ache, a gnawing emptiness that refused to be ignored.

Every evening, as the city lights flickered to life outside my window, I would sit by the same spot where we had shared so many intimate conversations. The quiet of the room would stretch on, filled with the echoes of laughter and shared secrets that now felt like distant memories. I would replay our last few conversations over and over in my mind, trying to pinpoint the exact moment things had begun to unravel. Was it something I had said? Something I had failed to say? The questions plagued me, unrelenting in their demand for answers.

I had always known that long-distance relationships were challenging, but nothing had prepared me for the relentless toll they would take on my sense of stability. The sporadic texts and brief phone calls seemed like fleeting glimpses of what we had once shared, but they did little to bridge the growing gap between us. Each conversation that ended with more silence in between felt like another step towards an uncertain future. It was as if we were drifting apart, our lives moving in different directions while we stood still, grasping at the fragments of what we had.

I tried to immerse myself in work, hoping it would distract me from the gnawing uncertainty. I took on new projects, poured myself into creative endeavors, but every shutter click, every image I captured felt incomplete without him. The photographs I once viewed as reflections of my soul now seemed like mere echoes of a time when everything was simpler, clearer. I found myself searching for him in every frame, hoping to find some semblance of the connection we had, but it was elusive, always just out of reach.

One particularly lonely evening, as I sat curled up on the couch with a blanket draped over my shoulders, I received a message from a friend. She had been a constant source of support through all the highs and lows, and her words of comfort were like a balm to my frayed nerves. She reminded me that the strength of our relationship would be tested by these very moments of doubt and distance. Her encouragement was meant to be uplifting, but it felt like a cruel reminder of the chasm that was growing between Liam and me.

I stared at the message, feeling the weight of her words but also the heaviness of my own heart. My thoughts were a tangled mess of longing and frustration, and I struggled to find solace in the platitudes offered by those who had never walked this path. The distance had become more than just a physical separation; it was now a barrier of emotions, of dreams and hopes that seemed increasingly distant.

As the days continued to pass, I found myself grappling with the harsh reality of our situation. The dream of a future together seemed to be slipping away, replaced by the stark reality of our separate lives. I wanted to believe that our love was strong enough to weather this storm, but every moment of silence and distance made it harder to cling to that belief. The fear of losing what we had built together began to overshadow my hope, and I was left with the painful task of trying to reconcile my feelings with the reality of our situation.

In the quiet of my apartment, surrounded by the remnants of a past filled with promise, I couldn't help but wonder if the end was near. The love that once felt so secure and unwavering now felt fragile, vulnerable to the forces of time and distance. It was a painful realization, one that left me questioning everything I had believed to be true. And as I faced the uncertainty of our future, I could only hope that, somehow, we would find a way back to each other, or at the very least, find peace in whatever outcome awaited us.

The night had settled over the city with its usual quiet hum, the kind that seems to wrap the world in a cocoon of solitude. My apartment, which had once buzzed with the energy of anticipation and possibility, now felt like a hollow echo chamber. I was lost in the monotony of my thoughts, the silence amplified by my uncertainty about Liam. The days without him had begun to stretch into an almost unbearable continuum, each moment feeling like an eternity.

It was on this particular night, while I was absorbed in trying to capture the essence of my melancholy through my camera lens, that the knock at my door came—a sudden, unexpected interruption in the steady rhythm of my loneliness. I stared at the door for a moment, wondering if it was just a figment of my imagination, a mirage born of my desperation for connection.

When I finally gathered the courage to open it, there he was. Liam stood on the threshold, his presence a stark contrast to the silence that had filled my space for weeks. He looked worn, the exhaustion etched into his features, but his eyes—oh, his eyes—still held that familiar, piercing intensity. It was as though he had traveled through time and distance, only to arrive at this very moment, at this very door.

"I couldn't stay away," he said simply, his voice a raw whisper that seemed to carry the weight of his struggle. The vulnerability in his gaze mirrored the emotions I had been grappling with. I could see it clearly now, the same uncertainty and fear reflected back at me, just as it had been that night on the terrace in Italy. It was both a comfort and a new kind of heartache, seeing him standing there, so close yet so distant from the person I had once known.

Without a word, I stepped aside to let him in, the familiar warmth of his presence flooding back into the room as soon as the door clicked shut behind him. There was a brief, poignant moment when we just stood there, taking each other in, before he reached for me. His arms wrapped around me, holding me tightly, and I could feel the tremor in his embrace, the way his body seemed to sag with relief and exhaustion.

"I've been scared," he admitted, his voice rough with a depth of emotion that spoke of long, sleepless nights and endless hours of introspection. "But being apart made me realize something—I don't want to lose you."

His words were like a balm to the doubt that had been festering in my heart. They were a tender reassurance, a bridge over the chasm of our separation. The knot that had tightened in my chest began to loosen, and for the first time in weeks, I allowed myself to believe that maybe, just maybe, we still had a chance.

We stood there in the quiet of my apartment, the only sounds the soft rhythm of our breathing and the distant city noise seeping through the windows. The relief of having him back, the sheer comfort of his proximity, was overwhelming. It was as though a part of me, long adrift, had found its way home. I could feel the walls I had built around my heart slowly crumbling, the defenses I had constructed in the wake of our separation starting to dissolve.

As I looked up at him, his face illuminated by the dim light of the hallway, I saw the man I had fallen for—the one whose presence had once felt like a promise of something beautiful and enduring. All the doubts, the fears, and the sleepless nights seemed to melt away, replaced by a fragile but hopeful sense of reconnection. I had missed him more than I had allowed myself to admit, and now, standing here with him in my arms, I felt a glimmer of the possibility that we could navigate this storm together.

He pulled back slightly, enough to look into my eyes with a sincerity that spoke volumes. "I know it's not going to be easy," he said, his voice trembling with the weight of his honesty. "But I want to try. I want us to figure this out, no matter how hard it gets."

The depth of his commitment was both comforting and daunting. I had longed for this moment, the one where our doubts and fears could be set aside for something more tangible. Yet, I knew that this was not the end of our struggles but rather the beginning of a new chapter filled with challenges and growth.

I took a deep breath, feeling the strength of his resolve blend with my own. "We'll figure it out," I whispered, the words carrying a promise and a plea all at once. "Together."

In that moment, standing there with Liam in my arms, I allowed myself to believe in the possibility of a future where we could rebuild what had been fractured. It was a fragile hope, but it was enough to carry us forward, one step at a time.

His arms around me were a lifeline, pulling me out of the dark sea of doubts that had been pulling me under. The weight of the silence between us seemed to evaporate with his touch, and I could almost feel the walls I'd built around my heart start to crumble. We stood there in the dim light of the hallway, clinging to each other as though our lives depended on it. The familiar scent of him—cedar and something faintly spicy—flooded my senses, grounding me in a reality I'd almost given up on.

For a moment, I closed my eyes, letting the rhythm of his breathing synchronize with my own. The fear and loneliness that had been my constant companions now seemed to dissipate in the warmth of his presence. His body pressed against mine felt like an anchor, holding me steady in a storm that had threatened to sweep me away.

"I missed you," I finally whispered, the words escaping from my lips as a fragile confession, heavy with the weight of all that had been left unsaid. He pulled back just enough to look into my eyes, his gaze softening. The intensity of his stare seemed to search for the truth of my feelings, to confirm that this reunion was as real as it felt.

"I missed you too," he said, his voice cracking with the sincerity of his confession. He reached up to brush a stray lock of hair from my face, his fingers lingering on my skin as if he needed to reassure himself that I was truly here. His touch was both tender and urgent, as though he feared that if he let go, I might vanish like a mirage.

We moved to the living room, the silence that followed filled with an unspoken understanding. He sat down on the couch, and I joined him, our knees nearly touching. We were close enough that I could feel the heat from his body, the comforting solidity of him beside me. I reached for his hand, intertwining my fingers with his, and he squeezed gently, as if trying to convey all the words he couldn't find.

"I've been trying to figure out what went wrong," I admitted, my voice barely above a whisper. "It felt like we were slipping away from each other, like I was losing you." The vulnerability in my voice was something I had been holding back for too long, but now it spilled out with an intensity that surprised me.

Liam's expression hardened, as though the weight of my words had struck a chord deep within him. "It wasn't supposed to be like this," he said, his voice tight with frustration. "I thought if I threw myself into work, I'd figure things out. But all it did was make me realize how much I need you." His eyes met mine, and there was a raw honesty in his gaze that cut through the fog of our misunderstanding.

I took a deep breath, trying to steady the emotions that were surging within me. "I've been afraid," I confessed, my voice trembling. "Afraid that maybe this was just a dream, something fleeting that wouldn't survive the reality of our lives." The admission felt like a release, a shedding of the layers of fear that had been building up inside me.

Liam's eyes softened with empathy, and he reached out to brush a tear from my cheek. "I don't want to lose you either," he said, his voice low and earnest. "Being apart made me realize just how much you mean to me. I was scared to admit it, scared to face the possibility that we might not make it. But now, seeing you here, I know I can't let this go."

There was a moment of silence as we both absorbed the gravity of his words. The past few weeks had been filled with so much doubt and distance, but now, in the quiet of this room, it felt as though we were rediscovering the connection that had drawn us together in the first place. I reached out to him, our fingers intertwining once more, and for the first time in weeks, I felt a glimmer of hope.

"I don't want to lose this either," I whispered, leaning into him. "But we have to be honest with each other, no more hiding behind work or silence." The words felt like a pact, a promise to face whatever came next together.

Liam nodded, his expression resolute. "I agree," he said, his voice steady. "Let's not let fear drive us apart. We need to face it head-on, together."

As he spoke, I felt a renewed sense of determination. The road ahead might be challenging, filled with obstacles and uncertainties, but the fact that he was here, that he had come all this way to find me, gave me hope. The night was far from over, and as we sat together, the promise of a new beginning began to take shape. It wasn't a guarantee of an easy path, but it was a chance—a chance that I was willing to fight for, no matter how difficult the journey might be.

His admission hung in the air between us, a fragile thread connecting our hearts in the midst of the chaos that had enveloped us. I could see the exhaustion etched into his features, the weariness that spoke of sleepless nights and days spent wrestling with his own doubts. My own heart ached for him, for the distance that had grown between us, for the silence that had come to define our relationship. But now, with him here, that silence was being replaced by something infinitely more precious: the truth.

"I've been struggling too," I confessed, my voice trembling as I tried to articulate the depth of my feelings. "I felt like I was losing you, like the person I thought I knew was slipping away." I could feel the tears pricking at the corners of my eyes, the raw emotion bubbling to the surface. I didn't want to cry, not now, not in front of him, but it was impossible to hold back the flood of feelings that surged through me.

Liam's gaze softened, his thumb gently brushing away the tears that had begun to escape. "I never wanted to hurt you," he said, his voice laden with remorse. "I thought I was protecting you from my own mess. But all I did was push you away." There was a vulnerability in his eyes that mirrored the pain I had felt, and it was in that moment that I realized we were both adrift in the same storm.

He reached out, cupping my face in his hands, his touch tender and reassuring. "I've been so focused on my career, on trying to make everything work, that I forgot what was truly important," he admitted. "You're what matters to me. More than anything." His words were like a balm to the wounds of my heart, soothing the doubts and fears that had taken root. I could see the sincerity in his eyes, the depth of his feelings, and it made me believe that maybe, just maybe, we could find our way back to each other.

We sat in silence for a while, the quiet of the room enveloping us like a cocoon. The warmth of his presence was a stark contrast to the cold emptiness I had felt in his absence. I leaned into him, resting my head on his shoulder, and he wrapped his arms around me, holding me close as if afraid I might vanish if he let go.

The familiarity of his embrace was comforting, a reminder of the connection we had shared. It was as if, in that moment, all the time we had spent apart melted away, leaving us with only the present and the future that lay ahead.

"I don't want to lose you either," I whispered, the words barely audible against the softness of his shirt. "But I need to know that we can make this work, that we can face whatever comes our way together." I felt his breath hitch as he absorbed my words, and he tightened his hold on me, his arms a fortress of strength and love.

"I'm willing to try," he said, his voice firm yet tender. "I'll do whatever it takes to make this work. To make us work." He pulled back slightly, enough to look into my eyes, and there was a determination in his gaze that gave me hope. The fear and uncertainty that had plagued me for weeks began to recede, replaced by a cautious optimism that perhaps we could overcome the obstacles that lay before us.

The night wore on, and we talked, our conversation a blend of confessions, apologies and promises. We shared our fears and hopes, laying bare the raw edges of our souls. It was a painful yet cathartic exchange, one that brought us closer together, mending the fractures that had formed between us.

As the hours passed, I felt a sense of peace settling over me, a quiet assurance that, despite everything, we had found our way back to each other. The road ahead would be challenging, filled with uncertainties and hurdles, but for the first time in weeks, I felt ready to face it. With Liam by my side, I believed that we could navigate the complexities of our lives and emerge stronger, more united than before.

When he finally stood to leave, the dawn's light beginning to filter through the window, there was a renewed sense of purpose in his steps. He leaned in and kissed me softly, a promise of things to come, and I felt a surge of hope that perhaps this wasn't just a fleeting moment of reconciliation but the beginning of a new chapter in our journey together.

Liam's visit marked the beginning of a delicate dance between hope and uncertainty. As we navigated the initial days together, it felt like we were walking on a tightrope, teetering between the past and an uncertain future. The familiarity of his presence was comforting, but the scars left by our separation were still fresh. Every glance, every touch seemed to hold a question—would this be enough to mend what had been broken?

Our mornings started with tentative smiles and awkward laughter, each of us trying to find a rhythm in our conversations that had once flowed so effortlessly. We would sit at the kitchen table, sipping coffee that had grown cold while we dissected our days, our fears, and our frustrations. It was a new kind of intimacy, one where every word was weighed carefully, and every silence spoke volumes.

The evenings were a bit easier. We would walk through the city, our hands intertwined, and the bustling energy of New York seemed to mask the quiet tension that lingered between us. The familiarity of the city, the streetlights casting their golden glow, felt like a balm to our wounds. Yet, each shared glance and soft touch was tinged with the lingering uncertainty of whether we could truly bridge the gap that had formed between us.

The nights were the hardest. We would lie side by side in bed, the space between us filled with unspoken words and unresolved doubts. The conversations about our future would stretch into the early hours of the morning, the weight of our commitment hanging heavily in the air. It was in these moments of vulnerability that I saw how deeply Liam cared, how he was grappling with his own fears and insecurities. His honesty was both reassuring and terrifying, a testament to how much we both wanted to make this work, even when it felt like we were stumbling in the dark.

We started making plans, talking about the future with a cautious optimism. There were discussions about moving, about finding a way to balance our careers and our relationship. Each conversation was a small victory, a sign that we were working together to build something lasting. But there were also moments of tension, where old arguments resurfaced and the reality of our separate lives clashed with our shared dreams.

One night, as we sat together on the rooftop of my apartment, watching the city lights flicker below, I could feel the weight of our struggles pressing down on us. Liam's hand was warm in mine, and the cool breeze of the evening seemed to whisper the promise of new beginnings. We talked about the fears that had plagued us, the insecurities that had crept into our relationship. There were tears and laughter, raw and unfiltered emotions that had been bottled up for far too long.

"I'm scared," I admitted, my voice trembling as I looked out at the sprawling cityscape. "Scared that we won't be able to make this work, that we'll fall back into the same patterns."

Liam's gaze was steady, his eyes reflecting a depth of emotion that made my heart ache. "I'm scared too," he said softly. "But I'm willing to fight for us. I'm willing to do whatever it takes to make this work."

His words were a balm to the doubts that had been festering in my heart. I could see the sincerity in his eyes, the determination to overcome the obstacles that lay ahead. It wasn't a guarantee of success, but it was a promise of effort and commitment, and that was enough for me to hold on to.

The days that followed were filled with small victories and setbacks, each moment a testament to our willingness to rebuild what had been broken. We celebrated the small achievements—the nights when we managed to talk without arguing, the days when we found joy in our shared moments. It was a process, one that required patience and understanding, but it was a process we were both committed to.

As we worked through our challenges, I began to see a future that was more than just a distant dream. It was a future built on trust and mutual respect, a future where we could navigate our fears and insecurities together. The road ahead was still uncertain, but with each step, I felt a renewed sense of hope.

Liam's visit had been a turning point, a reminder of the connection we shared and the strength of our bond. It wasn't a cure-all, but it was a beginning—a chance to rebuild and to grow. And as we continued to navigate the complexities of our relationship, I knew that as long as we were willing to fight for each other, there was still a chance for us to find our way back to the love we once knew.

Each day with Liam felt like an experiment in rebuilding something fragile but precious. The air between us was charged with a mixture of hope and apprehension, as if every word and gesture carried the weight of our collective uncertainties. We had these small, intimate moments that felt like glimpses of the past, but they were shadowed by the reality of our present situation. Sometimes, it was as if we were trying to piece together a jigsaw puzzle with missing pieces—there was progress, but we were never quite sure what the final picture would look like.

Our mornings were filled with attempts to recreate the ease we once had. We'd make breakfast together, the familiar clink of utensils and the smell of coffee filling the kitchen, but each glance or touch carried a hidden tension. It was a careful dance around our unresolved issues, each of us trying to find a balance between maintaining normalcy and confronting the lingering doubts.

One morning, as we cooked pancakes together, I noticed how Liam's movements seemed more deliberate, his laughter forced. I couldn't help but wonder if he was feeling the same weight of expectation that I was. It was as though we were both trying to navigate through a fog of what-ifs and maybes. Despite our attempts at normalcy, there was a lingering undercurrent of anxiety, a quiet question of whether we were merely delaying the inevitable.

In the afternoons, we'd venture out into the city, hoping that the change of scenery would help us find our rhythm. We'd walk through Central Park, trying to lose ourselves in the sprawling greenery and the energy of the city. The conversations during these walks were lighter, focused on the present, and for a moment, it felt like we were just two people rediscovering each other. But even in these moments of seeming ease, there was a persistent awareness of the underlying tension that clung to us.

Our evenings were when the real work began. As night fell and the city's lights twinkled outside, we'd sit on the couch, facing each other, and delve into the deeper issues that had surfaced during our time apart. These conversations were raw and often painful, but they were necessary. We talked about our fears of the future, our struggles with trust, and the challenges we faced in balancing our personal ambitions with our relationship. Each discussion felt like peeling back another layer of our complex feelings, revealing both the beautiful and the broken parts of us.

One night, after a particularly intense conversation about our future, Liam took my hand and looked at me with a mixture of vulnerability and determination. "I know we have a long way to go," he said, his voice steady despite the rawness in his eyes. "But I want to keep trying. I need you to know that you're not just a part of my life, you're a part of my future. I'm scared, but I'm more afraid of losing you."

His words, though simple, were profound. They were a testament to the effort he was putting into this relationship, despite the challenges we faced. It wasn't a guarantee of a perfect future, but it was a promise of commitment and willingness to work through the difficulties together. For the first time in weeks, I felt a glimmer of hope that maybe, just maybe, we could find a way to make this work.

Our nights were often filled with moments of reflection and tentative optimism. We would lie in bed, side by side, our fingers intertwined as we talked about our dreams and fears. These quiet moments were both comforting and unsettling, a reminder of how much we had to navigate but also of how much we cared for each other. The silence between us was no longer filled with doubt, but with a tentative peace—a space where we were both willing to confront the future together.

In the days that followed, we continued to make small strides, acknowledging that the road ahead was still fraught with challenges but also with possibilities. Our efforts to rebuild trust were ongoing, marked by both progress and setbacks. It was clear that the path to healing was not a straight line but a winding road filled with unexpected turns. Yet, despite the uncertainty, there was a renewed sense of commitment and a shared desire to create something meaningful out of our complicated reality.

We were still figuring things out, still learning how to navigate the delicate balance between our individual dreams and our shared future. But as we faced each day together, I couldn't help but feel that there was something profoundly real in our struggle—a testament to our willingness to fight for what we had, even when it seemed like the odds were stacked against us.

As the days passed, our efforts to mend the cracks in our relationship felt like climbing a steep, relentless hill. Every shared meal and walk in the park were small victories, but they didn't erase the struggles that had brought us to this point. It was in the quiet moments, the ones where words were unnecessary, that we felt the weight of our reality. Lying beside him in bed, I could feel the heat of his body against mine, but the space between us was palpable. It was as though we were both trying to grasp at something intangible, a past we couldn't fully reclaim but desperately wanted to.

One evening, as we sat on the couch, the city lights casting a soft glow over the room, Liam broke the silence. His voice was hesitant, as if he were choosing his words carefully. "I've been thinking," he started, his gaze fixed on a spot on the carpet, "about what we talked about earlier. About our future." His words hung in the air, and I felt a flutter of anxiety mixed with hope. We had discussed so many possibilities, but the reality of making them work felt daunting.

"I know," I replied softly, shifting to face him. "It's hard to imagine how we'll handle everything when we're so far apart. It's not just about us anymore—it's about our careers, our dreams, and how we fit together in all of that."

Liam looked at me, his eyes searching mine for something—reassurance, understanding, or perhaps both. "I've been scared," he admitted, his voice barely above a whisper. "Scared that I might be losing you, scared that the distance is too much for us to overcome."

I reached out and took his hand, feeling the warmth of his skin against mine. "I'm scared too," I confessed. "But I think what scares me more is the thought of not trying. We've come so far, and I don't want to lose what we have without giving it everything we've got."

We sat in silence for a few moments, holding onto each other, the weight of our shared fears mingling with the hope we had for our future. It was in these quiet moments that I felt the strength of our bond—the resilience that had carried us through so much already. We were both vulnerable, exposed, but we were also fiercely determined to make this work.

Later that night, as Liam fell asleep beside me, I found myself staring at the ceiling, my mind racing with thoughts and questions. How would we handle the reality of our careers pulling us in different directions? Could we build a life together despite the physical distance? The uncertainties seemed endless, but amidst them, I clung to the certainty of how much I cared for him. The past few weeks had been a trial, but they had also reinforced my belief in us.

The next morning, we decided to take a step back from our intense conversations and focus on enjoying our time together. We visited a local art gallery, something we used to do often when we first met. As we wandered through the exhibits, the familiarity of the experience brought a sense of normalcy and comfort. The paintings and sculptures were a distraction from our worries, a reminder of the simpler joys we had shared. For a while, the noise of our doubts quieted, replaced by the soft hum of shared appreciation and connection.

We ended the day with a quiet dinner at a cozy restaurant. The atmosphere was intimate, and as we talked about our favorite memories and the future we dreamed of, it felt like we were rediscovering each other. Our conversations flowed more easily, and for the first time in a long while, I felt a glimmer of the hope that had seemed so distant.

As Liam prepared to leave, we stood by the door, both of us knowing that this wasn't the end of our struggles but also recognizing that it was a step toward something better. "I'm not sure what the future holds for us," he said, pulling me into a heartfelt embrace. "But I do know that I want to keep trying. I want us to be part of each other's lives, no matter how difficult it might be."

I nodded, my heart full of both apprehension and hope. "Me too," I said, looking up into his eyes. "I want us to keep fighting for what we have. It's not perfect, but it's real, and that's worth everything."

As he walked away, I watched him disappear into the distance, feeling a bittersweet mix of emotions. It was a painful farewell, but it was also a promise—a promise that we would continue to fight for our relationship, no matter how hard the journey might be. And as I closed the door and turned back into the quiet apartment, I felt a small spark of hope ignite within me.

As the days rolled into nights and the nights into early mornings, our conversations took on a new urgency. The reality of what Liam had proposed began to settle in, each thought a blend of excitement and trepidation. I replayed our evening in my mind constantly, the soft glow of the bedside lamp casting long shadows that seemed to reflect the enormity of the decision we were facing.

It was a quiet Tuesday when Liam's proposal felt most real. We had spent the day going over plans and schedules, trying to piece together a semblance of how our lives would align. The sheer logistics of it were overwhelming—jobs, apartments, moving boxes, and the infinite small details that seemed to pile up with each passing hour. But it wasn't just the practical side of things that weighed heavily on me; it was the emotional depth of what we were contemplating.

One evening, as we sat at the kitchen table, the papers spread out before us like an uncharted map, I reached for Liam's hand. His touch was warm, grounding, and it brought a sense of calm to the whirlwind of thoughts racing through my head. "Do you really think we can do this?" I asked, my voice barely above a whisper.

Liam looked at me, his expression a mixture of determination and vulnerability. "I believe we can," he said firmly. "We have to. I know it's a lot to ask, and it's not going to be easy, but I'm willing to try if you are."

His words resonated deeply within me. We had always navigated our challenges together, and this was no different. The thought of uprooting my life, leaving behind the familiarity of my surroundings, was daunting. Yet, the idea of forging a future with Liam, of creating a space where we could grow together, was an intoxicating allure. The fear of the unknown was balanced by the hope of what could be.

That night, we talked long into the early hours, our voices hushed but filled with a newfound resolve. We discussed timelines, potential job opportunities, and the logistics of finding a new place to live. Each topic we broached seemed to solidify our decision, making the abstract concept of relocating feel increasingly tangible.

As we finalized our plans, we took solace in the fact that we were not alone in this journey. We were backed by the support of friends and family, whose encouragement helped to ease some of the anxiety we felt. Their belief in our relationship gave us strength, and their practical advice helped us navigate the complexities of the move.

A few weeks later, the day arrived for us to say our goodbyes. The process of packing up my apartment was bittersweet. Each item I packed held memories of my time in the city, but the excitement of the new chapter waiting for us made it easier to let go. Liam's presence was a constant source of comfort, his hand often resting on my back as we sorted through boxes and reminisced about our shared moments.

On the day we were set to leave, the streets of New York felt both familiar and foreign. There was a palpable sense of finality as we drove through the city, a feeling of leaving behind the life we had known for the promise of something new. Yet, the presence of Liam beside me, the shared glances and whispered reassurances, made the journey feel like an adventure rather than an ending.

We arrived at our new home with a mixture of exhaustion and exhilaration. The space was empty, save for a few essentials, but it held the promise of becoming our sanctuary. The process of unpacking and setting up our new life began, each box we opened bringing us closer to turning our house into a home.

As we worked side by side, the strain of the move and the weight of our decision seemed to lift. There were moments of laughter amidst the chaos, shared glances that spoke of our hopes and dreams.

We knew that the road ahead would be challenging, but we also knew that we were facing it together.

Liam and I took comfort in the fact that we had made this leap together, that we were committed to building a future where we could thrive both as individuals and as a couple. It was a new beginning, filled with promise and potential, and as we settled into our new home, we began to see the contours of the life we had envisioned. The road ahead was still uncertain, but with each passing day, we were learning to navigate it together, one step at a time.

In the weeks that followed, our lives seemed to revolve around the constant hum of packing tape and the soft murmur of moving boxes being filled. Each day brought its own set of challenges, from finding a new apartment to coordinating the logistics of relocating to a new city. It felt like we were living in a blur of activity, with every spare moment consumed by our growing list of tasks.

The transition from planning to action was a whirlwind, but there were also moments of unexpected calm. One afternoon, as I sat among a sea of cardboard and packing peanuts, I found myself reflecting on how this journey had unfolded. Liam was out meeting with potential employers, leaving me alone to tackle the endless pile of belongings that seemed to multiply with each passing hour.

Despite the busyness, there was an undeniable thrill that accompanied the uncertainty. It was the thrill of embarking on a new chapter, of building something together from the ground up. The fear of the unknown was tempered by the excitement of the possibilities that lay ahead. I often caught myself smiling at the thought of what our life might look like once we settled into our new home.

One evening, as I took a break from organizing the kitchen, I found a moment to breathe. Liam had returned from his meetings and was sitting on the floor surrounded by a stack of documents and a half-empty box of office supplies. His eyes met mine with a mixture of fatigue and determination. "We're getting there," he said with a tired smile.

I nodded, feeling a sense of shared accomplishment. "It feels like we're making progress," I agreed. "But it's also overwhelming."

Liam reached out, taking my hand in his. "I know it's a lot. But we're doing this together, and that makes it worth it." His touch was a reminder of the bond that had carried us through so much already. It was comforting to know that, despite the chaos, we were in this together.

As we continued to pack, our conversations often turned to our future. We talked about the small details that would make our new place feel like home—color schemes, furniture, and how we would rearrange our lives to fit into this new space. It was these conversations that made the abstract notion of relocation feel real and tangible. The idea of creating a home together was both exhilarating and daunting, but it was a challenge we were ready to face.

One night, as we collapsed into bed after a long day of moving boxes, Liam pulled me close. "I want you to know how much I appreciate everything you're doing," he said, his voice soft and sincere. "This is a huge step, and I'm grateful that you're taking it with me."

I could feel the weight of his words, the sincerity behind them. It was moments like these that made the struggles worthwhile, that reaffirmed why we were going through all of this. "I'm doing it because I believe in us," I whispered back. "And because I can't imagine doing it without you."

We lay there in silence, the hum of the city outside our window a constant reminder of the life we were about to begin. It felt as though the night itself was holding its breath, waiting for us to take the final leap. I could sense Liam's own anticipation, his eagerness to start this new chapter alongside me.

In the midst of the chaos, there was a sense of clarity that emerged. The journey to this point had been filled with uncertainties and obstacles, but it had also been marked by moments of profound connection and growth. As we prepared for this next big step, I realized that our love was stronger than the challenges we faced. We were building a future together, one step at a time, and that was something worth fighting for.

And so, as the moving boxes piled up and the days grew shorter, I held on to the promise of what lay ahead. Each box packed and each decision made brought us closer to the life we envisioned. The road was still uncertain, but the path was becoming clearer, and with Liam by my side, I felt ready to face whatever came next.

As the days passed, the intensity of our new reality began to settle in. The sheer volume of tasks felt overwhelming, but there was a peculiar comfort in the routine of it all. The boxes were a constant reminder of our impending transition, each one a vessel carrying pieces of our old life into the unknown. It wasn't just about moving possessions; it was about moving ourselves into a future that, while uncertain, felt promising.

The evenings were often the hardest. After long days of organizing and sorting, the quiet of our temporary apartment would set in. We'd sit together on the floor amidst the clutter, our conversations growing quieter, more introspective. It was during these moments that the gravity of our decision weighed most heavily on us. The excitement of the move was always tempered by the realization of what we were leaving behind. Our old routines, the familiarity of our surroundings, and the ease of established friendships seemed to drift further away, like a distant shore growing hazy in the twilight.

Yet, each time we spoke about our plans, the nervousness in our voices was replaced by an unwavering determination. We talked about the small things that would make our new place feel like home—the kind of art we'd hang on the walls, where we'd place our favorite pieces of furniture, and how we'd set up our cozy reading nook by the window. These discussions were more than just logistics; they were about building a life together, one that reflected both our dreams and our reality.

Liam's presence was a steady anchor throughout the chaos. His commitment to making this work was evident in every decision he made, every late-night conversation we had. There were moments of doubt, of course. Times when the weight of our decision felt almost unbearable, and we'd question whether we were making the right choice. But those moments were fleeting, overshadowed by the reassuring strength we found in each other. Our shared vulnerability, our fears, and our hopes became the foundation upon which we were building our future.

One particularly clear evening, as we took a rare break from packing to enjoy a quiet dinner, Liam looked at me with a sense of calm determination. "I know this isn't easy," he said, his gaze steady. "But I keep thinking about how far we've come. How much we've grown, both individually and together. And I believe that this—moving forward together—is the next step we need to take."

His words were a balm to my restless heart. I could see the sincerity in his eyes, the resolve that mirrored my own. It was then that I realized how deeply intertwined our lives had become. The uncertainties of our future no longer felt like obstacles but rather opportunities to build something meaningful and lasting.

We continued to plan, to dream, and to build. Every day brought us closer to the reality of our new life, and with each step, we grew more confident in our choice. It wasn't about the grandeur of the move or the excitement of a fresh start; it was about the quiet certainty that we were making the right decision for us. Our future, with all its challenges and possibilities, was taking shape before our eyes, and it felt like the beginning of something beautifully new.

As we lay in bed that night, the sounds of the city outside mingling with the hum of the air conditioner, I felt a profound sense of peace. The chaos of the move, the doubts, and the uncertainties were all part of the journey, but they were also part of the growth we were experiencing together. We weren't just moving to a new place; we were moving forward in our lives, hand in hand, ready to face whatever came next with the same strength and love that had brought us this far.

In those quiet moments, wrapped in the warmth of Liam's embrace, I knew that our future was no longer just a distant dream. It was unfolding in front of us, one day at a time, and it was exactly where we were meant to be.

As excited as we were about the prospect of a future together, the reality of making it happen was harder than we anticipated. Liam's career demanded constant travel, and my photography business was taking off in ways I hadn't expected. We were pulled in different directions, and balancing our ambitions with our relationship was proving more difficult than either of us had imagined. There were days when I questioned whether we had made the right choice, whether love was enough to bridge the distance between us. But every time we hit a rough patch, we reminded each other of what we had fought so hard to build. We weren't willing to give up that easily.

The first month after moving was a whirlwind. The apartment, though our sanctuary, was still a jumble of unpacked boxes and half-formed plans. Each morning, we faced the disarray of our new life, trying to balance setting up home with the demands of our respective careers. The challenge of establishing routines that worked for both of us seemed almost insurmountable at times. Liam's schedule was erratic, with flights and meetings that stretched late into the night. My days were filled with photoshoots and editing sessions, and the tension between our conflicting schedules often left us feeling drained.

The phone calls became lifelines, but even they couldn't always bridge the gap between our realities. We'd talk for hours, sharing snippets of our days, the small victories and frustrations, but sometimes it felt like we were grasping at shadows of the intimacy we used to share. The moments of connection were fleeting, often overshadowed by the mundane stressors of everyday life. There were evenings when we'd finally settle down after a long day, only to find ourselves too exhausted to really talk or connect.

One night, as I was working late into the evening, editing a series of photos for an upcoming exhibition, Liam called. His voice was tight with exhaustion, and I could hear the weariness in every word. "I'm sorry I've been so distant," he said, his tone heavy with regret. "This schedule is killing me, and I hate that it's affecting us."

I felt a pang of sadness at his words, mixed with my own frustration. "I know," I replied softly. "It's just hard. I feel like we're losing the closeness we had."

We talked through the discomfort, and as always, we came out on the other side more connected, if not entirely resolved. It was in these conversations that we found our strength—by confronting the difficulties head-on and making the effort to understand each other's struggles.

The weekends became our refuge. We'd use the precious time together to rediscover the joy we had in each other's company. We explored the city, taking long walks through parks and along the waterfront, finding solace in the quiet moments we could carve out from our busy lives. It was in these simple acts of togetherness that we found a rhythm, a way to navigate the turbulence of our new life.

Yet, even with these efforts, there were days when the challenges seemed overwhelming. I would catch myself staring at the framed photos of us from our time in Italy, remembering the ease and happiness we had shared. The contrast with our current struggles felt stark, and it was hard not to let doubt creep in. Was this new chapter worth the sacrifices we were making?

During these times, Liam and I would talk through our fears, often sitting together on the couch, holding hands as we laid out our concerns. Our discussions were raw, filled with the kind of honesty that only comes when you're truly vulnerable. We talked about our future, our dreams, and the fears we had about maintaining a relationship under such pressure.

"I'm scared," I admitted one evening, my voice barely above a whisper. "Scared that we're not going to make it through this."

Liam squeezed my hand, his eyes reflecting the same fear I felt. "Me too," he said. "But I believe in us. I believe in what we have. We just need to keep fighting for it."

There were no easy answers, no guarantees of a smooth path ahead. But in those moments of doubt, the commitment we had to each other became our anchor. We weren't perfect, but we were willing to face our challenges together, to navigate the rough patches with as much love and understanding as we could muster.

Each day, we worked to build a life that could accommodate both our ambitions and our relationship. It was a continuous balancing act, but it was one we were both determined to make work. The road ahead was uncertain, filled with obstacles and hard decisions, but as long as we faced them together, we knew we had a fighting chance.

It was on a chilly Thursday evening, as I sat at the kitchen table sifting through a stack of paperwork, that the weight of our situation truly settled over me. Liam was in another time zone, again, and our conversations were confined to brief texts or hurried phone calls that never seemed to last long enough. I missed the sound of his laughter, the warmth of his touch, and the way he'd look at me with that mix of affection and amusement that made me feel like I was the center of his world.

As the days grew colder, our challenges seemed to intensify. The apartment, once a beacon of our fresh start, felt more like a reminder of our struggle. Every empty corner, every half-finished project, was a testament to the dreams we were striving to make a reality. I spent my days juggling photoshoots, deadlines, and the constant stream of emails that seemed to increase with each passing day. Nights were consumed by editing sessions that stretched into the early hours. I longed for the solace of Liam's presence, but his career kept pulling him away.

One particular night, after a long and exhausting day, I finally managed to take a moment for myself. I curled up on the couch with a cup of tea, trying to relax, when my phone buzzed. It was a message from Liam: "I miss you. Let's have a real conversation tonight. I need to hear your voice." I sighed with relief, a small smile tugging at my lips. We had been so caught up in the whirlwind of our individual lives that we hadn't had a proper, uninterrupted conversation in weeks.

When the time came for our call, I settled into the couch with my tea and dialed his number. His face appeared on the screen, and for a brief moment, it felt like no time had passed at all. But as we started to talk, I realized how much we had both changed in our time apart. Our conversation began with the usual pleasantries, but soon the façade crumbled.

"I don't know how we're supposed to keep doing this," Liam admitted, running a hand through his hair. "It feels like we're both running in different directions and barely managing to stay on the same path."

I nodded, understanding more than he knew. "I feel the same way. It's like we're so focused on making everything work that we're forgetting why we're doing it in the first place."

The vulnerability in his eyes mirrored my own fears. We spoke candidly about our frustrations—the missed anniversaries, the nights spent alone, the ever-growing list of things left unsaid. It was a raw conversation, one that left us both feeling exposed, but it was also a necessary one. It was a reminder that we had to fight for each other, that our love was worth the struggle, even if it didn't always feel like it.

Liam reached through the screen, his hand almost touching mine. "I'm so sorry for being absent. I know it's not fair to you, and I wish I could be there more."

My heart ached at his words, not out of resentment, but from the shared understanding of our predicament. "It's not just about being there physically," I said softly. "It's about being present, and sometimes it feels like we're both just existing in the same space but not really connecting."

He nodded, his expression thoughtful. "We need to find a way to reconnect, to make time for each other despite everything. Maybe we can schedule regular times to talk or even set aside days where we focus solely on us, no work, no distractions."

The idea was both comforting and daunting. The logistics of our lives seemed so complicated, but the thought of having a plan to prioritize our relationship was a glimmer of hope. We both agreed to try, to make a conscious effort to build a routine that allowed us to be more than just voices on a phone.

As the call ended, I felt a renewed sense of determination. We had a long road ahead, filled with obstacles that would test our commitment and patience. But hearing Liam's voice, seeing the earnestness in his eyes, reminded me of why we were making these sacrifices. Our love wasn't just a fleeting moment—it was something we had built together, something worth fighting for.

Liam and I were far from perfect, but we were learning to navigate the complexities of our lives with honesty and resilience. The challenges we faced were significant, but they also presented an opportunity for growth. We were finding our way, step by step, and though the path ahead was uncertain, I knew that as long as we faced it together, we could overcome anything.

We both knew that the path we had chosen was fraught with hurdles, but in that moment, as I stared at Liam's face on the screen, I realized how desperately we both wanted to make it work. He looked tired, his eyes shadowed by exhaustion, and I could see the same determination in him that I felt within myself. It was a quiet, unspoken understanding that despite the chaos and the distance, our bond was stronger than the trials we faced.

"I feel like we're always playing catch-up," I confessed, my voice breaking slightly as I tried to hold back tears. "Every time we manage to get a handle on one part of our lives, another challenge comes up. It's like we're constantly fighting to keep our heads above water."

Liam nodded, his face reflecting my frustration. "I know. It feels like every time we have a moment of clarity, something shifts, and we're back to scrambling. I hate it. I hate that I'm not there with you, that I can't be a part of your everyday life. I miss the small things—the way you laugh when I tell a terrible joke, the way you look when you're lost in thought over a new project."

His words hit me like a wave, washing away some of the doubts and fears that had accumulated. "I miss that too," I admitted. "I miss you. I miss us being able to just be. Sometimes, I wonder if we're asking too much of ourselves, trying to juggle everything and still stay connected."

"But we're not," Liam said firmly, his voice taking on a note of resolve. "We're not asking too much. We're just asking a lot from ourselves, from each other. And that's okay. It's part of the process. We knew it wasn't going to be easy. If anything, this makes me more certain that we're doing the right thing. If we can make it through this, through all the obstacles, then we can make it through anything."

His confidence was a lifeline, pulling me from the brink of despair. I took a deep breath, letting his words sink in. "You're right. We knew this was going to be tough, and we knew there would be times when it felt like it was all falling apart. But we also knew that we loved each other enough to fight through it."

There was a pause, and then Liam's eyes softened. "I've been thinking about what we can do to make things better. Maybe we need to be more deliberate with our time, plan our visits more carefully, make sure we're both on the same page about what we want and need from each other.'

I nodded, a glimmer of hope flickering within me. "Yes, I think that would help. I need to feel like we're both invested in this, not just separately but together. Maybe setting some clear goals for our time together and our individual pursuits could give us a better sense of direction."

Liam smiled, a small, weary but genuine smile. "I'd like that. I'd like to know that we're working towards something concrete, that there's a plan. It gives us something to look forward to, something to hold on to when things get tough."

We talked for hours, mapping out ideas and making tentative plans. It was a relief to voice our concerns and hopes openly, to address the elephant in the room with a shared sense of purpose. By the time the call ended, I felt a renewed sense of connection and optimism. We were still miles apart physically, but emotionally, we were navigating this journey together.

As I set my phone down and prepared for bed, I realized that while the challenges were daunting, our commitment to each other was unwavering. We might not have all the answers or a clear path laid out, but we had each other's hearts, and that was a powerful foundation. The road ahead was uncertain, but I was ready to face it, knowing that Liam and I were in it together, every step of the way.

As I sat on the edge of our bed, staring at the email on my phone, I could hardly believe what I was reading. The words seemed to blur together, the implications of Liam's offer overwhelming every other thought. A long-term contract in Europe—an opportunity that seemed tailor-made for him, a dream job that could elevate his career in ways we had only imagined in passing conversations. But as exciting as it was, it was also a stark reminder of the distance that had always threatened to pull us apart.

Liam was out in the living room, pacing like a caged animal. The energy in the apartment felt charged, each of us silently grappling with the weight of this decision. I could hear the soft thud of his footsteps, each one echoing my own internal struggle. I wanted to go to him, to wrap him in my arms and offer some comfort, but I was too absorbed in my own turmoil to move.

When he finally walked into the bedroom, his face was a mask of conflicted emotions. "Have you read it?" he asked, his voice barely above a whisper.

I nodded, swallowing hard. "I've read it. It's... it's incredible. You've worked so hard for this."

Liam's eyes searched mine, a mixture of hope and dread flickering in their depths. "I don't know what to do, and I'm terrified of making the wrong choice. This could be everything I've ever wanted professionally, but it also means being apart from you again."

The vulnerability in his voice was almost more than I could bear. I had seen him at his strongest, his most confident, but this moment laid bare his fears and uncertainties. It mirrored my own—an intricate dance of dreams and reality, of love and ambition. My heart ached at the thought of him leaving again, but I also knew how much this opportunity meant to him.

"I'm scared too," I admitted, my voice trembling. "Scared of what this means for us. It's not just the time apart—it's the emotional distance that comes with it. We've struggled so much already, and I don't want to lose what we've worked so hard to build."

Liam came closer, sitting beside me on the bed, his hand finding mine. "I don't want to lose us either. But I also can't ignore how big this opportunity is. I've dreamed about working in Europe, about growing in my career, and this is my chance. I don't want to make a decision that will haunt me."

I squeezed his hand, trying to steady my racing thoughts. "And I don't want you to regret your choices either. I want you to have everything you've ever dreamed of, but I also want us to find a way through this. I don't have all the answers, Liam. I just know that whatever we decide, it needs to be something we can both live with."

We sat in silence, the weight of the decision pressing down on us like a heavy fog. Each possibility seemed to swirl around us, creating a dizzying array of outcomes that felt equally daunting. The idea of him leaving again felt like a cruel repetition of our past struggles, but turning down the offer seemed like denying him a chance he might never get again.

"I've been thinking," I finally said, my voice soft but firm, "about what this could mean for us. Maybe there's a way to make it work. Maybe it's not about choosing one thing over the other, but finding a balance. We've always managed to adapt, to make things work even when it seemed impossible."

Liam's gaze was intense, filled with a mix of relief and apprehension. "What do you mean?"

"I mean," I said, taking a deep breath, "that maybe we should explore how we can support each other through this. Maybe we can look into ways of keeping our connection strong even when we're apart. We've done it before; we've found ways to make our relationship work despite the challenges. It won't be easy, but I believe we can figure it out."

Liam's expression softened, a small, hopeful smile playing at his lips. "You really think so?"

"I do," I said, my voice growing steadier. "I think if we face this together, if we commit to making it work, then we can find a way through. We just need to be open and honest with each other, to keep communicating and supporting each other no matter what."

For the first time since he received the offer, Liam seemed to relax, a semblance of peace settling over him. "Okay," he said softly, "let's take this one step at a time. Let's figure out how to make it work, and we'll handle whatever comes next together."

The decision wasn't made, and the future remained uncertain, but in that moment, I felt a glimmer of hope. The road ahead would be challenging, but at least we were facing it together, committed to finding a way to bridge the gap between our dreams and our love. And for now, that was enough.

Liam's hand tightened around mine, his thumb brushing absentmindedly against my palm. His gaze was fixed on the wall, as though he could find the answers etched into its plain surface. The silence in the room was heavy, punctuated only by the occasional creak of the floorboards beneath his restless steps. I wanted to offer solace, to reassure him that whatever decision we made would be the right one because we'd made it together. But the uncertainty gnawed at me too, a relentless whisper that refused to be ignored.

"I don't want to lose you," Liam said finally, breaking the silence. His voice was strained, as if admitting this fear was as hard as making the decision itself. "But I also don't want to give up on this chance. It's everything I've worked for, everything I've dreamed about."

I understood the gravity of his words. This opportunity wasn't just another job offer—it was the culmination of years of hard work, late nights, and sacrifices. I had seen him push through the toughest moments, his dedication unyielding. It was his chance to shine, to prove to himself and the world what he was capable of. The thought of him walking away from it seemed impossible, yet the thought of losing him again was equally unbearable.

"It's not just about this opportunity," I said softly, trying to steady my voice. "It's about what it means for us. We've been through so much, and every time we get close to making it work, something pulls us apart. I don't want us to be a series of missed chances and regrets."

Liam turned to face me, his eyes reflecting the same vulnerability I felt. "I know. I keep thinking about how we've managed to get through the hard times before. Maybe we can find a way to make this work too. But... what if this is too much?"

I squeezed his hand, willing my own fears into silence. "We've always found a way. It's never been easy, but we've never given up on each other. Maybe this is another test, another chance for us to prove that we're stronger than the challenges that come our way."

Liam nodded, though the lines of worry on his face remained. "It's just hard to see past the immediate obstacles. I want to take this job. I want to succeed and make something of myself, but I also want us to be okay. I want to have both, but it feels like something has to give."

His struggle mirrored my own. I had my own dreams, my own aspirations that were taking off in unexpected ways. The photography business that had started as a passion project was now blossoming into something much bigger. It was exhilarating, but it also meant more time commitments, more responsibilities. The idea of putting my career on hold to accommodate another separation felt like sacrificing a part of myself.

"What if we tried something different?" I suggested, my voice tentative. "What if we looked at this as an opportunity for growth, both for our careers and our relationship? Maybe there's a way to support each other while still pursuing our individual dreams."

Liam's gaze softened, and he let out a sigh. "What do you have in mind?"

"I don't know exactly," I admitted. "Maybe it's about setting clear boundaries and expectations, finding ways to stay connected even when we're apart. We can make plans to visit each other, schedule regular video calls, and focus on the positives. We can figure it out as we go, instead of letting the fear of the unknown dictate our choices."

He seemed to consider this, the tension in his shoulders easing slightly. "That sounds... possible. I want to believe that we can make it work. I just don't want to feel like we're constantly fighting against the odds."

"Neither do I," I agreed. "But we've faced so many challenges together, and we've come out stronger each time. Maybe this is another one of those moments. Maybe we just need to trust in what we have and believe that we're capable of overcoming this too."

Liam's hand slipped from mine as he stood up and walked to the window, looking out into the city below. The streetlights cast a soft glow, and the city seemed alive with possibilities. I watched him, hoping that whatever decision we made would bring us closer to the future we both wanted.

After a long pause, he turned back to me, his expression resolute. "Alright. Let's talk to each other openly and honestly. Let's set a plan in motion and see where it takes us. I don't want to let fear or uncertainty dictate our choices."

I stood up and walked over to him, my heart swelling with a mix of relief and determination. "Agreed. We'll figure it out together. Whatever happens, we'll face it as a team."

He pulled me into an embrace, and for a moment, everything felt right. The uncertainties of the future seemed to recede, replaced by the reassurance of our shared commitment. The road ahead might be fraught with challenges, but for now, we were facing them together, ready to carve out a path that honored both our dreams and our love.

The days that followed were a blur of sleepless nights and heavy conversations. We tried to distract ourselves with ordinary things—grocery runs, the occasional movie night, and even a few attempts at cooking together—but the weight of the decision loomed over everything, a dark cloud that refused to dissipate.

One evening, as I watched Liam make dinner, the familiar rhythm of his movements offered a strange comfort. The clinking of utensils, the sizzle of vegetables in the pan—these sounds, once so mundane, now felt like the anchor we needed amidst the storm. I leaned against the kitchen counter, my gaze fixed on him, trying to memorize the contours of his face, the way his brow furrowed in concentration. It struck me how much I took these moments for granted before, how the simple act of sharing space and time together was so profoundly significant.

"Do you remember when we first started dating?" Liam's voice broke the silence, gentle and reflective. "I used to think that if we could just make it through the little stuff, the big stuff would be easier. But now, it feels like we're facing everything at once."

I nodded, my throat tight. "I remember. We had our share of problems, but they always seemed manageable. This... this feels different. It's like we're at a crossroads, and every path has its own set of consequences."

He turned to face me, his expression earnest. "I don't want to make a decision that's going to tear us apart. But I also don't want to look back and regret not taking this opportunity. I've worked so hard for this, and it's everything I've ever wanted professionally."

The kitchen was filled with the aroma of cooking, but it was the silence between us that tasted bitter. I felt a pang of frustration, a mix of hope and hopelessness swirling inside me. We had fought so hard to find our way back to each other, and now it felt like we were being pushed apart again by forces we couldn't control.

"We've always managed to find a way through," I said, trying to infuse my words with conviction. "Maybe we need to think about this differently. What if instead of seeing this as an end, we view it as another challenge we have to face together?"

Liam paused, the spatula in his hand stilling mid-air. "You think we can make it work even if we're apart for so long?"

I sighed, a sound of both resignation and resolve. "I think we owe it to ourselves to try. We've already proven that we're capable of overcoming obstacles. Maybe this is just another one of those tests. We need to be honest with each other about what we want and how we can support each other, even when we're miles apart."

He looked at me, his eyes softening with the realization of what I was suggesting. "You're right. We've always been stronger together. Maybe the distance won't be as insurmountable if we keep communicating, if we keep finding ways to stay connected."

We stood there in the kitchen, the tension between us easing as we began to accept the reality of our situation. It was clear that the path ahead wouldn't be easy, but there was a sense of purpose in our decision-making. We were no longer just reacting to circumstances; we were choosing to face them together, even if it meant navigating new, uncharted territories.

As we finished dinner, Liam reached out and took my hand, his touch warm and reassuring. "Whatever happens, I want you to know that I'm committed to making this work. I'm willing to face the challenges, no matter how daunting they seem."

I squeezed his hand, feeling the sincerity in his words. "And I'm committed to supporting you, no matter where this journey takes us. We'll find a way to make it work, just like we always have."

The promise of our shared future, despite its uncertainties, felt like a beacon in the fog. It wasn't a guarantee of ease or perfection, but it was a commitment to each other and to the love that had always guided us through the darkest times. As we sat down to eat, the warmth of the meal and the quiet strength of our conversation gave me hope that, no matter how the road ahead unfolded, we would face it together.

The night before Liam had to make his decision was one of those rare moments when time itself seems to stand still, holding its breath in the quiet. The room was draped in shadows, punctuated only by the soft glow of the bedside lamp, casting a gentle light on the tangled mess of our emotions. We sat on the edge of the bed, our fingers brushing together, a small, almost futile gesture of comfort that seemed to highlight the chasm growing between us.

The silence stretched, heavy and oppressive, each minute a reminder of the enormity of the choice before us. Liam's shoulders were hunched, a stark contrast to the confident and dynamic presence I had come to know. His face, usually so expressive and animated, was now drawn tight with an intensity that mirrored my own internal struggle.

I had spent the entire day wrestling with my thoughts, trying to come up with a way to ease the pain of this moment, but no amount of reasoning could change the harsh reality. His opportunity in Europe was more than just a job; it was a culmination of years of hard work and sacrifice, a chance to finally step into a role he had dreamed of for so long. Turning it down would mean losing something he had built with his own hands, a piece of his heart that he had poured into his career.

Yet, the other side of the coin was just as daunting. The idea of facing another long stretch of time apart, of navigating the maze of our lives without the immediate comfort of each other's presence, felt like a burden too heavy to bear. The thought of watching him leave, knowing that the next time we would be together would be marked by months of separation, was a pain I could hardly fathom.

Finally, I gathered the courage to speak, though my voice was barely above a whisper. "You have to take it," I said, each word feeling like it was being torn from me with great effort. The admission felt like a betrayal, a knife twisting in my heart as I realized that I was pushing him away, even as I wanted nothing more than to keep him close.

Liam turned to me, his eyes glistening with unshed tears, reflecting a pain that mirrored my own. His hands, usually so steady and sure, trembled slightly as he reached for mine. "I don't want to lose you," he said, his voice breaking under the weight of his emotions. "But I can't turn this down. Not after everything."

His words were a balm and a wound all at once. They spoke of his commitment to his dreams, to the future he had envisioned for himself. Yet, they also underscored the depth of the sacrifice he was about to make, the cost of choosing his career over the life we had begun to build together. It was a heart-wrenching choice, one that felt like it would fracture us beyond repair.

As we sat there, our hands intertwined, I felt a rush of love mixed with sorrow. The decision wasn't just about choosing between two paths; it was about acknowledging that our love was strong enough to withstand the distance, but not without its own set of challenges. We were on the brink of another chapter in our story, one that would test us in ways we had never imagined.

The air was thick with unspoken promises, the weight of the decision hanging over us like a cloud that refused to lift. We both knew that this wasn't the end, but rather a new beginning fraught with its own set of trials. The choice to let him go was a testament to our commitment to each other, a promise that despite the miles and the months apart, we would find a way back to one another.

With a sigh that seemed to release all the tension of the past hours, Liam pulled me into a tight embrace. I could feel his heartbeat against my own, a rhythmic reminder of the love that had brought us to this point. "We'll make it work," he whispered into my hair, his breath warm against my skin. "We have to."

I nodded against his chest, the tears I had been holding back finally breaking free. "We will," I said, my voice muffled. "We'll fight for this. For us."

The room fell silent again, but this time, it was a silence filled with a fragile sense of resolve. We knew that the road ahead would be difficult, that the separation would test our strength and our love. But we had made our choice, and with it, we had also made a commitment to face whatever came our way with courage and determination.

As I looked up at him, I saw not just the man I loved, but also the reflection of the future we were both willing to fight for. The decision had been heartbreaking, but it was a testament to the depth of our bond. Even as we faced another period of uncertainty, we held on to the hope that our love would see us through.

His words, raw and edged with pain, seemed to reverberate through the silence between us, their weight pressing down on my chest like a physical force. I could see the struggle in his eyes, the conflict between what he wanted and what he felt he needed to do. Every inch of him seemed to be pleading with me, and I wanted to reach out and take away his torment, even as I knew that was impossible.

"I don't want to lose you," he said again, this time his voice cracking, breaking under the strain of his emotions. I could see the sincerity in his gaze, the desperation that spoke of his love for me and the internal battle he was fighting. It was as if he was trying to reconcile the dream he had worked so hard for with the reality of the life we had built together, a life that was now hanging in delicate balance.

I took a deep breath, trying to steady the tremor in my own voice. "I know," I managed to say. "I know how much this means to you. And I... I don't want to be the reason you turn it down." My heart felt like it was being pulled in a million different directions, each thread a reminder of the sacrifices we were both being asked to make. I wanted to be supportive, to encourage him to chase his dreams, but the reality of what that meant for us was almost too much to bear.

We sat there, our hands clasped together as if the simple touch could bridge the distance between our hearts. The room felt unbearably small, the walls closing in as if they were pressing us towards the inevitable conclusion we both feared. It was in these moments of raw vulnerability that the gravity of our situation hit hardest.

Liam shifted, his face buried in his hands for a moment as he tried to collect himself. "How do we do this?" he asked, his voice muffled but still trembling. "How do we survive another year apart? I want this, but I don't want to lose us in the process." The anguish in his voice was palpable, a reflection of the depth of his love for both his career and me. It was a delicate balance, one that neither of us had the answer to.

I wished I had the perfect words, some magical phrase that could make everything clear and simple. But instead, all I had was the truth, and that truth was that love, no matter how powerful, couldn't always solve every problem. Sometimes, it required more than just words; it required action, sacrifice, and a willingness to endure the hardships that came with following one's dreams.

"We'll have to find a way," I said softly, my voice steady despite the turmoil inside. "We've faced challenges before, and we've always come through them. This... this is just another challenge. We'll have to lean on each other more than ever, and it won't be easy. But if we're committed to making it work, then we'll find a way."

Liam looked up, his eyes meeting mine with a mixture of hope and fear. The resolve in his expression was tempered by the uncertainty of what lay ahead, but there was a flicker of something more—an understanding that, despite everything, we were in this together.

"We'll have to be strong," he said, his voice more certain now. "We'll have to trust that this time apart will make us stronger, not weaker." His words, though heavy with the burden of what was to come, were also filled with a commitment that couldn't be ignored. It was as if he was trying to convince both of us that this was the right choice, even as his heart ached with the thought of leaving.

We held each other, the warmth of our embrace a small comfort in the face of the overwhelming decisions that lay before us. The night was long, filled with quiet conversations and the occasional tear, but through it all, there was an unspoken agreement between us. We had chosen to fight for our love, to believe that no matter how difficult the road ahead might be, we could face it together.

As the first light of dawn began to creep into the room, casting a pale glow over our weary faces, I felt a strange sense of calm settle over me. It wasn't the end of our story, just another chapter—one that we would navigate with all the strength and love we had. And though the path was uncertain, the decision we had made was one that, for now, gave us both the courage to face whatever came next.

The weight of our decision settled heavily in the room, an almost tangible presence that seemed to seep into every corner of our lives. The finality of it all was overwhelming, but beneath the surface of our sorrow, there was a strange, bittersweet clarity. We knew this was the right choice, even if it was the hardest one we had ever faced.

As we lay in bed that night, the silence between us was both comforting and painful. Liam's breathing was steady but shallow, a stark contrast to the turbulent storm within me. I traced my fingers lightly over his chest, feeling the steady rise and fall beneath my touch. Each breath felt like a reminder of the love we were trying so desperately to hold onto, even as circumstances threatened to pull us apart.

His hand found mine in the darkness, squeezing it gently as if to reassure himself that this was real, that we were still here, still connected despite the decisions we had made. "We're going to be okay," he said softly, his voice a comforting murmur in the quiet. I wanted to believe him, to cling to the hope that our love would be enough to carry us through the next year. But the reality of our situation loomed large, casting long shadows over our future.

"I hope so," I replied, my voice trembling slightly. "I really hope so." There was a heaviness in the air, a mix of fear and longing that seemed to wrap itself around us like a shroud. I could feel the tremors of uncertainty beneath the surface of his calm facade, and I wished there was something more I could do to ease the burden of this decision.

In the days that followed, the reality of Liam's impending departure became more and more real. We spent our time together savoring every moment, every touch, every shared laugh and quiet conversation. It was as if we were trying to freeze time, to hold onto the fleeting moments of togetherness before the inevitable separation. We made plans for regular visits, for video calls and handwritten letters, for any way we could find to bridge the distance that would soon separate us.

Despite the preparations, the looming sense of loss was almost too much to bear. Every goodbye felt like it carried the weight of an eternity, every embrace a reminder of the preciousness of the time we had together. We clung to each other, finding solace in our closeness even as we knew it was only temporary.

On the day of Liam's departure, the finality of our decision hit me with a force that left me breathless. We stood at the airport, our hands intertwined, our gazes locked as if trying to memorize every detail of each other's faces. The moment was a mixture of sorrow and hope, a poignant reminder of the love we were fighting to preserve despite the miles that would soon stretch between us.

"I'll be back," Liam promised, his voice steady but filled with emotion. "We'll get through this. I know we will." His words were meant to comfort me, to reassure both of us that this was just another hurdle in our journey. But beneath the surface, I could see the same uncertainty reflected in his eyes, the same fear of what the future held.

"I know," I replied, trying to muster a smile even as my heart ached. "Just promise me you'll take care of yourself." It was a small plea, a reminder that even though we would be apart, we were still connected by the bond of our love and the commitment we had made to each other.

With a final, lingering kiss, he walked towards his gate, his figure slowly disappearing into the crowd. I watched him go, my heart heavy with the weight of our decision and the uncertainty of the days to come. The space beside me felt emptier than ever, a stark reminder of the distance that would soon separate us.

As I made my way back to the car, the reality of the separation settled in, a sobering reminder of the challenge we had chosen to face. But even amidst the pain and the sorrow, there was a flicker of hope, a belief that our love was strong enough to withstand the trials ahead. We had chosen to fight for us, to hold onto the dreams we shared despite the obstacles. And that, in itself, was a promise of the future we both still believed in.

# Chapter 10:

The days seemed to blur into one another, each one a repetition of the last as I settled into my new routine. I'd wake up with the city's heartbeat pulsing through my apartment—honking cabs, distant sirens, the murmur of countless lives intertwining. Yet, despite the vibrant chaos of New York, the absence of Liam made it feel as though a crucial element of my life was missing. The space where he used to be was now filled with an emptiness that no amount of bustling city noise could mask.

When I'd sit down to work on my photography, I'd often find myself lost in thoughts of him, my mind drifting to the little things that made him uniquely him. How he'd wrinkle his nose when he was thinking deeply, or the way he'd bite his lower lip when he was trying not to smile too broadly. I'd look at my phone, scrolling through our old texts and photos, trying to hold onto the moments we shared. Each snapshot of his smile was a reminder of the happiness we'd once known together, and each message a thread that kept us connected across the miles.

The calls were our sanctuary, moments where time seemed to stretch and contract in miraculous ways. I'd find myself waiting in anticipation for the small screen to light up with his name, each ring of my phone sending a thrill through my heart. Our conversations would start with the mundane—the weather, the workday, the small victories and frustrations. But as the minutes stretched, the small talk would give way to deeper conversations, the kind that pulled us closer together despite the physical distance.

One evening, as we lay on our respective beds in different time zones, the quiet between us was filled with unspoken understanding. Liam's voice came through the speakers, softened by the weariness of his travels. "I miss you," he said, his words barely a whisper but heavy with emotion. I closed my eyes, imagining his hand reaching through the screen, bridging the gap between us. "I miss you too," I replied, my voice trembling as I tried to keep my composure. "Every single day."

We talked about our future, dreams and plans that seemed both tangible and elusive. We spoke of the day when we wouldn't have to rely on screens and messages to feel close. We planned trips, discussed where we might live, and even laughed about the small things we'd do together. Those conversations were our anchor, keeping us grounded in the belief that this distance was only a temporary obstacle in a much larger journey.

Still, there were days when the weight of our separation felt almost unbearable. On those days, I would retreat into my work, focusing on my photography as a means of escape. The lens became my ally, capturing moments of beauty and distraction that helped to soothe the ache of missing him. Each photo I took was a reflection of my own emotional landscape, a visual representation of the love and longing that colored my life.

The simple pleasures we once took for granted—morning coffee together, lazy weekend afternoons—now felt like distant memories, sweet yet sorrowful. I'd catch myself daydreaming about the next time we'd be together, about the feel of his arms around me, the sound of his laugh filling the room. Those dreams were a bittersweet comfort, a reminder of what we were working toward and a balm for the loneliness that sometimes crept in.

Even with the challenges, there were also moments of unexpected joy. I'd receive a surprise package from Liam—perhaps a book he thought I'd enjoy, or a handwritten letter that smelled faintly of his cologne. Each gift was a piece of him sent across the miles, a reminder that despite the distance, he was always thinking of me. I'd run my fingers over the paper, feeling connected to him in a way that no phone call or text message could replicate.

As weeks turned into months, our love continued to evolve, adapting to the constraints of our new reality. The distance, though difficult, had a way of highlighting just how much we meant to each other. It was in the small gestures—the thoughtful messages, the shared dreams, the quiet moments of understanding—that we found our strength. We knew that this was just another chapter in our story, one that tested our commitment and deepened our bond.

The knowledge that we were working toward a future together, despite the obstacles, gave me the courage to face each day with hope and resilience. We were navigating uncharted waters, but our love was the compass that guided us. In the end, I believed that no matter how far apart we were, our hearts would always find their way back to each other.

The days grew into weeks, and the weeks into months, each one a testament to our resolve and love. We fell into a routine that, while not ideal, became our lifeline. I'd wake up early and start my day with a rush of excitement, knowing that each new sunrise brought me closer to the next call with Liam. I would grab my phone, eager to see his name light up the screen, a beacon of normalcy amidst the chaos of our separate worlds.

Our video calls were more than just a means of communication; they were moments of intimacy carved out from the vast expanse that lay between us. I would sit in my favorite corner of the apartment, the sunlight filtering through the curtains, and he'd be in his own small corner of Europe, bathed in the soft glow of his desk lamp. It was during these calls that the distance between us seemed to shrink, if only for a little while. We'd laugh about the little things, share stories of our days, and let our worries unravel in the comfort of each other's company.

There were times when the distance felt like a physical weight pressing down on me, making my chest ache with longing. On those nights, when the city lights were my only company, I'd pull up our old photos, letting the memories wash over me. I'd remember the way his eyes crinkled when he laughed, the warmth of his embrace, and the way his hand felt in mine. These memories were my solace, a reminder of the love we had and the promise we made to endure.

One rainy evening, as I watched the droplets race down my windowpane, I received a message from Liam that was unlike any other. He'd sent me a photo of a quaint little café he had stumbled upon, with a handwritten note tucked inside a cup of coffee. The note read, "I found this place, and it made me think of you. I can't wait to bring you here one day." It was a simple gesture, but it spoke volumes. It was a promise of the future we both longed for, a future where the distance between us was nothing more than a memory.

Despite our efforts to stay connected, there were moments when the separation seemed unbearable. I'd find myself sitting in our favorite café in New York, the seat across from me empty and cold. I'd imagine him there, smiling at me, the way he used to, and it would take everything I had not to break down. But then I'd remember his voice, the way he'd encourage me to stay strong, to keep moving forward, and I'd pull myself together.

In the quiet moments, when the city was asleep and the apartment was still, I'd think about our future. The plans we made seemed both incredibly close and heartbreakingly far away. We talked about where we would live, the life we wanted to build together, and the small, mundane things that would make up our days. These conversations were my anchor, a reminder that our love was a constant, unwavering force, even if our lives were in flux.

The time apart was not without its challenges, but each hurdle we overcame made our connection stronger. Every call, every message, every shared moment was a testament to our commitment. I'd find comfort in the fact that no matter how far apart we were, our love was a thread that wove us together, keeping us close even when we were miles apart.

As the months passed, I started to see the end of this long-distance chapter on the horizon. It was a distant, shimmering line, but it was there, and it was growing closer with each passing day. I knew that when Liam returned, we would have a new understanding of each other, a deeper appreciation for the time we spent together, and a stronger bond forged through the trials we faced.

And so, each day, I embraced the distance with a mixture of hope and resilience. I kept our shared dreams in the forefront of my mind, letting them guide me through the lonely nights and the challenging moments. We were building something beautiful, something worth every bit of effort and sacrifice, and that thought kept me going, day after day.

A year passed, and Liam's contract in Europe finally ended. The day he returned to New York, I was waiting for him at the airport, my heart pounding with anticipation. Every moment of our long-distance journey had led up to this one, and as I stood in the crowded terminal, all I could think about was the moment I would see him again.

The airport was a whirlwind of noise and movement, but none of it mattered. My gaze was fixed on the arrivals gate, scanning the faces as they came into view. The world seemed to blur around me, the cacophony of luggage wheels and chatter fading into the background. I felt as if time had slowed, each second stretching out as I waited for the one face that would make everything right.

Then, through the sea of people, I saw him. Liam emerged from the gate, his eyes searching, and when they finally met mine, everything else fell away. There was a moment, just a heartbeat, where it felt like we were the only two people in the room. I could see the exhaustion in his eyes, but also the relief and joy that mirrored my own. My breath caught in my throat as he moved towards me, the intensity of the moment making it feel like the ground had shifted beneath us.

When he reached me, his arms enveloped me in a hug so warm and familiar that it felt like coming home after a long journey. I buried my face in his chest, inhaling the scent that I had missed so dearly, and I felt tears prick at the corners of my eyes. "I'm home," he whispered against my hair, his voice thick with emotion. I pulled back slightly to look at him, my heart swelling with the realization that this was real, that we had finally made it through the hardest part.

We didn't need words at that moment; our embrace spoke volumes. The trials of the past year—the endless video calls, the lonely nights, the uncertainty—were all worth it for this moment of pure, unfiltered joy. I could see the strain in his face, the tiredness from a year of working away from home, but it was overshadowed by the love that shone in his eyes. His hands cupped my face gently, his touch reassuring and tender.

As we walked out of the airport together, hand in hand, the weight of the past year seemed to lift. The future stretched out before us, a blank canvas waiting to be filled with our dreams and plans. The noise of the airport faded behind us, replaced by the quiet comfort of our shared presence. We spoke of mundane things, the kind of everyday chatter that somehow felt profoundly significant. We talked about the city, the changes it had undergone in his absence, and the small things that had become routine in my life without him.

The drive home was filled with an easy companionship, a natural rhythm that had never truly disappeared despite the distance. We slipped into our old routines with surprising ease, the familiarity of our shared space wrapping around us like a favorite blanket. It was as if we had never been apart, and yet, I knew that we were different now—stronger, more resilient, and deeply appreciative of the time we had together.

That evening, as we settled into our apartment, it felt like we were stepping into a new chapter of our lives. The space was filled with the scent of home-cooked meals and the soft glow of warm lighting. We unpacked his bags together, laughing at the small souvenirs he had collected during his travels, each one a testament to the adventures he had experienced while we were apart.

Later, as we lay in bed, the quiet of the night enveloping us, I looked over at Liam and felt a profound sense of peace. We had faced the challenge of distance and come out stronger on the other side. The journey hadn't been easy, but it had been worth it. And as I felt his hand clasp mine in the dark, I knew that no matter what challenges lay ahead, we would face them together—stronger than ever before, with a love that had only deepened with time and trials.

With Liam home and the promise of our future stretching out before us, I couldn't help but feel a renewed sense of hope and excitement. The road ahead was ours to navigate, and I was ready to face it with him by my side. As I drifted off to sleep, I held onto the certainty that we were finally where we were meant to be, and that the best was yet to come.

The airport seemed to hum with a new energy as we walked through the sliding doors, the cold New York air greeting us like a long-lost friend. Liam's hand was firmly wrapped around mine, his grip both reassuring and invigorating. Every step we took felt like a testament to our resilience, a tangible marker of the journey we had navigated together despite the distance that had separated us.

We ventured through the bustling airport, making our way to the parking lot where I had parked. The city lights of New York sparkled in the distance, and it struck me just how vibrant and alive everything seemed, as if mirroring the renewed hope in my heart. As we approached my car, Liam paused for a moment and looked around, a look of wonder on his face.

"This place feels different," he said, his voice filled with awe. "I've missed it."

I smiled, squeezing his hand. "And I've missed you. Every corner of this city reminds me of you."

He turned to me, his eyes reflecting the streetlights and the deep emotions that had been building over the past year. "I didn't realize how much I missed everything until now."

We settled into the car, the familiar hum of the engine a comforting sound after so many months apart. The drive home was filled with easy conversation, the kind that flowed naturally when two people are just happy to be together again. We talked about everything and nothing—the little details of our daily lives, the trivial moments that felt so significant now that we could share them in person. It felt as if we were reclaiming our shared narrative, weaving together the threads of our separate experiences into a cohesive story that belonged to us both.

The drive was short, but it gave me time to reflect on how much had changed. My apartment, once a place of solitude, now felt like a beacon of our future together. When we arrived, I unlocked the door and we stepped inside, the familiar smell of home wrapping around us. I looked at Liam, his expression a mix of curiosity and contentment as he took in the space he hadn't seen in so long.

"Let me show you around," I said, eager to share the little updates and changes I had made.

As we moved through the apartment, I could see the joy in his eyes as he took in the personal touches I'd added. He seemed genuinely impressed by the small changes—how the living room had been redecorated, the little touches in the kitchen that made it feel more like a home. It was as though he was seeing our life together for the first time again, and it was both exciting and reassuring.

After the tour, we settled on the couch, Liam's arm draped around me as we sat close, savoring the closeness we had yearned for.

The evening was calm, the city sounds filtering through the windows, creating a soothing backdrop. We talked about our plans, the dreams we had put on hold, and the future we wanted to build together.

"Do you remember when we first talked about moving in together?" Liam asked, his voice soft as he traced patterns on my arm.

I nodded, my heart fluttering at the memory. "I do. It feels like so long ago, but it's always been there, that desire to build a life together."

Liam looked at me with a gaze that held both determination and affection. "I want to make that happen. I want us to have a real home, a place where we can both settle and dream and live."

The words filled me with a deep sense of fulfillment. We had faced so many challenges, and the promise of a future together now seemed so tangible, so possible. It was the culmination of everything we had worked for and sacrificed, and the realization of our shared dreams.

We spent the rest of the evening talking about our plans—where we wanted to live, the kind of home we imagined for ourselves, and the life we hoped to create. The conversations were filled with laughter and excitement, and the night felt like a celebration of our reunion and the future that lay ahead.

As the hours passed and we finally drifted off to sleep, wrapped in each other's arms, there was a profound sense of peace. The future, with all its uncertainties and promises, felt like a vast, open field, and we were ready to walk it together. In the quiet of the night, with Liam's steady heartbeat beside me, I knew that no matter what challenges lay ahead, we would face them as one, stronger and more united than ever before.

The apartment was bathed in the soft glow of evening light as we settled in, the quiet comfort of home embracing us after the whirlwind of our reunion. Liam wandered through the rooms, his gaze lingering on the small changes I'd made—the new art on the walls, the plants that had grown lush in his absence. It was as though he was rediscovering a part of his life that had been on hold, waiting for him to return.

"Everything looks amazing," he said, his voice filled with genuine appreciation. "You've made it so warm and inviting."

I watched him, feeling a mixture of pride and relief. "I wanted to make it a place we'd both be excited to come back to. It's not just my home anymore—it's ours."

He turned to me, his eyes soft with emotion. "I've missed this. I've missed us."

We settled on the couch, a place that had once been so familiar but now felt new and precious. Liam's presence was a balm to my soul, a reminder of all the things I had held onto while he was away. We talked for hours, recounting stories of our days apart, laughing over the mundane and the extraordinary. Each word exchanged was a bridge reconnecting us, rebuilding the closeness we had fought so hard to preserve.

As the night wore on, the city outside became a backdrop to our renewed intimacy. We found ourselves wrapped in each other's arms, the weight of the past year melting away. The comfort of being physically together again was more profound than I had anticipated. The little things—his touch, his warmth, the way his breath felt against my skin—reminded me of how deeply I had missed him.

"You know," Liam said softly, his voice a soothing murmur in the quiet of the night, "I never realized how much I relied on these moments with you until I was away."

I nestled closer to him, feeling the steady rhythm of his heartbeat. "We've both learned a lot about ourselves this year. About what we're willing to sacrifice and what we're willing to fight for."

He stroked my hair, a gentle gesture that spoke of love and commitment. "I wouldn't have made it through without you. Your letters, your calls—they kept me going."

We stayed like that for a while, wrapped in each other's embrace, savoring the simple pleasure of being together. The challenges of the past year felt distant now, overshadowed by the certainty of our reunion. In that moment, the world outside faded into insignificance. All that mattered was the warmth of Liam's arms around me and the promise of a future we would build together.

As the clock ticked past midnight, we finally pulled away from each other, our eyes meeting in the dim light. There was a shared understanding between us, a silent agreement about what lay ahead. We were ready to face whatever came next, not as two separate individuals, but as a united front.

"I'm excited about our future," I said softly, my heart swelling with hope. "Whatever it brings."

Liam smiled, his eyes reflecting the same sentiment. "Me too. I know it won't always be easy, but I'm ready to face it all with you."

He kissed me then, a kiss that spoke of everything we had endured and everything we hoped to achieve. It was a promise, a declaration that we were stronger together than we had ever been apart. And as we finally settled into the quiet of the night, with the city's distant hum serving as a lullaby, I felt a profound sense of peace.

No matter what challenges lay ahead, we had navigated the hardest part. Our love had not only survived the distance but had thrived in it. And now, as we looked towards the future, I knew that with Liam by my side, we could face anything. We had found our way back to each other, and this time, we were ready to build a life that was truly ours, together.

Milton Keynes UK
Ingram Content Group UK Ltd.
UKHW031902260924
448786UK00001B/84

9 798227 963444